COPYRIGHT

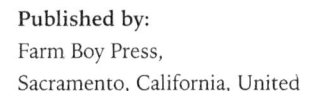

Published by:
Farm Boy Press,
Sacramento, California, United

First electronic edition: April, 20..
This edition: April 16, 2021

Copyright © 2021 by Lila Dubois, all rights reserved.

Cover design by Lila Dubois
Copyedits by Fedora Chen
Book formatted by Farm Boy Press

ISBN: 978-1-941641-59-0 ebook
ISBN: 978-1-941641-61-3 paperback

Without limiting the rights under copyright reserved above, no part of this publication may be reproduced, stored or introduced into a retrieval system, or transmitted, in any form or by any means (electronic, mechanical, photocopying, recording, or otherwise), without the prior written permission of both the copyright owners and the above publisher of this book, except for the use of brief quotations in a book review.

Publisher's note:
This book is a work of fiction. The names, characters, places, and incidents are products of the writer's imagination or have been used fictitiously and are not to be construed as real. Any resemblance to persons, living or dead, actual events, locale or organizations is entirely coincidental.

This ebook is licensed for your personal enjoyment only. It may not be re-sold or given away to other people. If you would like to share this book with another person, please purchase an additional copy for each recipient. If you're reading this book and did not purchase it, or it was not purchased for your use only, then please purchase your own copy. Thank you for respecting the hard work of this author.

ALSO BY LILA DUBOIS

Orchid Club

The San Francisco Trilogy

San Francisco Longing

San Francisco Lost

San Francisco Love

The Paris Trilogy

Paris Pleasure

Paris Punishment

Paris Promise

The Vienna Trilogy

Vienna Betrayal

Vienna Bargain

Vienna Bliss

Masters' Admiralty *Erotic Ménage Romance written with* **New York Times** *bestselling author Mari Carr*

Treachery's Devotion

Loyalty's Betrayal

Pleasure's Fury

Honor's Revenge

Bravery's Sin

The Trinity Masters, *Erotic Ménage Romance written with* **New York Times** *bestselling author Mari Carr*

Elemental Pleasure

Primal Passion

Scorching Desire

After Burn (free short story)

Forbidden Legacy

Hidden Devotion

Elegant Seduction

Secret Scandal

Delicate Ties

Beloved Sacrifice

Masterful Truth

Fiery Surrender

The Trinity Masters: Volumes 1-4

Warrior Scholars - Trinity Masters Novellas

Hollywood Lies

Joyful Engagement

BDSM Checklist, BDSM Erotic Romance

Writing as L DuBois

A is for…

B is for…

C is for…

D is for…

E is for…

F is for…

G is for…

H is for…

I is for…

J is for…

K is for…

L is for…

M is for…

N is for…

Undone Lovers, *BDSM Erotic Romance*

Undone Rebel

Undone Dom

Undone Diva

Undone Toy

Standalone BDSM Erotic Romance

Betrayed by Love

Dangerous Lust

Red Ribbon

The Glenncailty Ghosts, *Modern Gothic Romance*

Redemption

Lovers

Ghosts

Bones

The Wraith Accords

Carnal Magic

City of Angels, Supernatural

Writing as E.M. Nally

Faith of Beasts

Monsters in Hollywood, *Paranormal Romance*

Dial M for Monster

My Fair Monster

Gone with the Monster

Have Monster, Will Travel

A Monster and a Gentleman

The Last of the Monsters

Standalone Paranormal Romance

Briar Rose

Calling the Wild

Kitsune

Sealed with a Kiss

Standalone Shifter Romance

His Wolf Heart

Savage Satisfaction

Zinahs, *Fantasy Romance*

Forbidden

Savage

Bound

CONTENTS

N IS FOR...
L. DUBOIS

Chapter 1	3
Chapter 2	11
Chapter 3	19
Chapter 4	29
Chapter 5	35
Chapter 6	47
Chapter 7	57
Chapter 8	63
Chapter 9	77
Chapter 10	89
Chapter 11	101
Chapter 12	111
Chapter 13	121
Chapter 14	133
Chapter 15	145
Chapter 16	153
Chapter 17	159
Chapter 18	167
Epilogue	179
A note from Lila…	183
About the Author	185

N IS FOR...

L. DUBOIS

CHAPTER 1

Well that was...utterly insane.
Autumn followed the other subs away from the large barn the overseers of the club ostentatiously called the Conclave. Though the phrasing was far more accurate than referring to the building as an actual barn.

Before the Las Palmas property—named for the palm trees that lined the driveway—had been secretly converted into LA's most exclusive BDSM club, and christened Las Palmas Oscuras, it had been an equestrian estate. The barn, covered arena, and various outbuildings were a reminder that it had once been used to stable and train expensive horses, owned and ridden by the uber-wealthy who lived in and around Malibu and the canyons.

She still didn't think of herself as one of them.

Not horse people, nor pretentious Malibu Hills people.

But she was now one of the uber-wealthy.

When she was at work she owned it, but times like this the label didn't sound right, or feel right. Imposter syndrome was real. People who were used to having money acted, and reacted, different. Since her high personal net worth was a relatively recent development, she didn't always react like a rich person.

And right now, she was the only one who seemed flabbergasted by what had just happened.

She was fighting the urge to shout, "What the *actual* fuck just happened?"

There weren't even what-the-fuck expressions on the other subs' faces. The few low-voiced conversations she could hear lacked the outraged tone she would be using if she opened her mouth.

Autumn hiked up the top of her corset, though that was more out of habit than because it needed adjusting. Scarlet satin with black lace might be a bit obvious for sexy apparel, but she liked bold colors, and this particular corset had industrial-level boning in the front which kept her boobs in place.

She shivered. It was just before sunset, and the walk from the Conclave back to the main building complex over the well-landscaped grounds of the estate was a little chilly. It wasn't cold out, but the location wasn't tropical either, so wandering around in a corset and a teeny, stretchy skirt left a lot of skin exposed to the cooling air of late afternoon.

She'd be warm as soon as they were back in the main complex. Most of the club was kept heated, including the outdoor courtyards.

"Autumn?"

She stopped in her tracks, shocked to hear her name. The speaker had a smooth, masculine voice.

Luckily, she was at the back of the crowd, and the woman directly behind her changed course in time to avoid a crash.

Turning on her heel, Autumn faced the speaker.

Brown-haired with light colored eyes—in this light they could have been blue or gray—he was good looking in the generic way that made her think of East Coast Ivy League men who came from old money and denied their own privilege. He was taller than her by an inch or two, and wore a well-tailored suit. That was hardly unexpected among the Doms at Las

Palmas. With monthly dues in the five figures, only very financially successful or independently wealthy people could afford to be members.

Plus, you had to be kinky as fuck.

Autumn gave him a second once over, her blood heating as she contemplated just what sort of kinks the suit and solid veneer of respectability were hiding.

"That's me." She raised both hands in a little "ta da" gesture.

He smiled, and ohhh baby. That was some smile.

The man held up a large envelope. "I recognized you from the picture."

"Picture? Wait, is that from this bat-shit insane game?" She pointed first at the envelope he held aloft and then back at the Conclave.

"It is, and we're partners." The smile grew. He had two perfect smile lines that bracketed his mouth.

"I just got a weird flashback to high school and having to talk to someone I didn't know because we'd been assigned as lab partners."

He laughed, a good, genuine sound, and then held out a hand. "I'm Daniel."

His hand was warm compared to her cold fingers.

"I'm Autumn. Though you obviously already know that."

"May I walk you back?" Daniel offered his elbow.

Autumn slipped her fingers around his forearm. "Why, thank you. Very kind."

They started walking, with enough space between them that her shoulder only occasionally brushed his arm, but she could just about feel the warmth of his body along her side.

There was a unique delight in meeting a new BDSM partner. About making small talk with someone who would soon put their hands on her naked body. Pleasure her, hurt her, in all the right ways.

It was a bit like picking up a guy in a bar for a one-night

stand. Looking around in the dim light and seeing someone. Going to talk to them, starting with inane conversation, all the while knowing where it was going.

But at Las Palmas, meeting someone new was actually less dangerous than picking someone up at a bar. There was less chance of being murdered, since all members were thoroughly vetted. And, most importantly for her, the kink element was guaranteed.

"Bat shit," Daniel said, surprising her.

"Huh?"

"You called the game 'bat shit'. I like it. Not a phrase I hear often."

Autumn stopped walking, pulling her hand free of his arm. Daniel turned to her, brows raised.

"Are you one of those stuffy, high-protocol, formal tops?"

The hint of a smile touched his mouth and the smile line on the left side of his mouth appeared. "And if I am?"

Her stomach tightened with anxiety, but she didn't let any of it show. "Then we're going to have a rough time."

"Because you dislike high-protocol?"

"And I curse like a sailor. Pleasure, pain... Both best expressed with cursing."

Daniel's smile grew. "I'm not stuffy, or formal."

"Really, cufflinks, you're not formal?"

He raised his arm, twisting it to look at the silver cufflink which was just peeking out from the bottom of his jacket sleeve.

He frowned. "Oh dear, these are my gardening cufflinks. How embarrassing. Please ignore these and pretend I'm wearing the solid gold and diamond ones."

Autumn let out a peal of laughter so loud that she startled even herself. She slapped a hand over her mouth to dampen the sound as Daniel dropped the faux-chagrin and smiled at her.

When she'd calmed herself, Autumn dropped her hand.

"Okay, fair enough. I shouldn't judge a book by its very nice cover—"

"Thank you." He bowed with a little flourish.

"—and I'm sorry in advance for my language."

Daniel smiled at her, and started to offer his arm, then stopped, and instead removed his suit jacket. She was about to make a joke about getting naked, but he stepped close, draping his coat over her shoulders. It was warm from his body heat and smelled good. Male and expensive. The faintest trace of cologne.

Her sassy comment died on her tongue. She gently gripped the edges of the coat, pulling it a little tighter against her skin. He was standing close enough that she had to tip her head back just a little to look up at him. "Thank you."

Gray. His eyes were the gray of smoke and coastal fog.

"You're welcome." He'd lowered his voice in apparent deference to their proximity, and it added an intimacy that made her very, very aware of exactly how little she was wearing.

It was thrilling and terrifying to look up into this man's eyes and know that though they were strangers, they were about to share something very physical.

She wanted to kiss him.

That thought had her mentally, if not physically, backpedaling. Autumn slapped on a saucy grin. "Well, partner, what's our letter?"

Daniel's gaze searched her face, and his expression was all too serious. It was a penetrating stare that made her feel like he could see inside her. Not her thoughts, or not *just* her thoughts, but into her heart, her soul, where she kept her old hurts, and barely healed emotional scars.

She looked away. Not down, but off to the side.

He stepped back and then motioned with one hand for her to precede him. His serious, knowing expression was gone, the grin back in place. It was enough to make her wonder if she'd imagined that searching look.

She hadn't. The butterflies in her stomach confirmed that. As did the heavy arousal that heated her blood and made her hyper-aware of her half-exposed breasts and rapidly dampening thong.

She started walking, and he fell in step beside her. There was no one else near them. The last of the subs had disappeared through the opening that would take them through the interconnected buildings back to the gate of the Subs' Garden. There were several men behind them—other Doms who, like Daniel, already had their assigned letters for the checklist game—but they were far enough back that their presence didn't break the sense of intimacy between them.

When they reached the building complex, Daniel paused.

"Where would you prefer to talk? The library, or perhaps the dining room?"

"I haven't eaten dinner yet." She glanced behind them to the northwest, where the sun would soon sink into the Pacific Ocean, though the ocean itself wasn't visible from here. "But it's still early."

"I could eat." Daniel smiled.

"Says the person not wearing a corset." She rapped her knuckles against her stomach.

"Would you like to change first?"

Yes, because discussing a scene and getting to know a new play partner were things best done when comfortable and able to focus. Wearing a corset was both less than totally comfortable and too much of a reminder that she was the submissive.

She should say yes and go change into a robe. Or maybe a bralette and booty shorts, if she still wanted to be cute and sexy, but not so tightly confined.

What came out of her mouth was, "No, I'll be fine...if you'll help me loosen it a little?"

The way he inhaled, the fire that ignited in his eyes, made her shiver with desire.

"It would be my pleasure," he murmured.

This time he put his hand on the small of her back as he guided her towards the club's dining room.

As they reached the door Daniel paused again, looking down at her, his smile lines peeking out. "Our letter is N. I hope you don't have any objections to nipple play."

CHAPTER 2

The dining room was empty, and the buffet laid out though the dishes were all still covered. She stood beside Daniel and stared at the untouched buffet.

"We could start with a drink." Her reluctance to be the first one to dig in was probably stupid. She had just as much right to the fancy buffet food as anyone else—she paid her dues—but the idea of being the first one to eat made her vaguely uncomfortable.

"Food first, so we both have time to digest," Daniel countered.

He picked up a plate and looked back at her. "May I make you a plate?"

She could do it herself, but that would be hard to do if she also wanted to keep his jacket around her shoulders. She liked the smell of his cologne too much to give it up.

And this was the place where no one would think less of her for allowing herself to be taken care of.

"Yes, thank you."

Daniel smiled, then started reading off the small placards in front of each dish. She went for some roasted veggies and half a piece of pecan encrusted fish as well as a scoop of wilted spinach salad.

He put far more food on her plate than she would eat, and then carried it not to one of the tables, but to one of the sunken seating areas. He set down her plate and a napkin-wrapped roll of silverware before holding out a hand, offering it to her for support as she descended the steps.

She reluctantly took off his jacket, laying it out neatly on the padded bench, before taking her seat. Daniel came back several more times, carrying first his own plate, then wine bottles and glasses.

"Red, white, or bubbles?"

What she really wanted was a mimosa. She had the palate of a child when it came to booze, preferring sweet and bubbly. Not that she would ever admit to that here, or really anywhere but the privacy of her own home where she would occasionally make herself a pitcher of mimosas with low calorie orange juice and a ten dollar bottle of brut from the grocery store.

Then she'd drink a cheap, low-calorie mimosa while sitting in her multi-million dollar condo, on a couch that cost as much as normal people's first cars.

She leaned forward—as much as the corset would allow—to look at the labels of the bottles. She knew good wine, and when in public was just enough of a wine snob to fit in with her co-workers. "I do love an off-dry Riesling."

Daniel opened the wine and poured them each a glass.

She was glad he didn't make a production of it, and when he passed her a glass she raised it out of habit. He picked up his own, touching it to hers with a small clink.

They each took a sip, and the wine was buttery and sweet. It warmed her, but not the same way his gaze did. She felt his attention sliding down her exposed skin, lingering on her plumped breasts above the top of the corset.

"Can I help you with that?" Daniel set down his glass and gestured to her midsection.

Autumn worried the inside of her cheek with her teeth for a moment.

"If you'd prefer we talk before I touch you in any way, or if you'd like me to find someone else…" He let the words trail off.

"I'm not nervous," Autumn insisted. Then she shook her head. "That was a very stupid thing to say. Of course I'm nervous."

Daniel nodded, his expression serious. "And I respect that."

"But I would like the corset loosened before I try to eat anything." She pushed to her feet, and scooted around the low table until she was beside Daniel.

He remained seated, a move she thought was deliberately meant to make her feel more comfortable.

She turned her back to him, pulling her hair forward over her shoulder, though it wasn't long enough to really be in the way.

"The ties are in the middle, tucked in under the edge." She twisted to look back at him, but it strained her neck so she stopped.

"A properly laced corset," he murmured. She felt a small tug as he dug the tails of the laces out. The material of the corset was too thick for her to feel his touch, and she resented the garment because of it.

There was an audible creaking sound as he undid the knots of the upper lace, which started at the top of the corset and ended half way down, right at her natural waist.

She took a deep breath, deliberately expanding her chest as the corset loosened. She expected him to add even more slack to the lacing, but instead she felt a tug as he tied the cording once more.

"That's it?" She twisted to look back at him again. All she could see was the top of his head.

The corset creaked as he untied the lower lace. This one he loosened much more than he had the upper half, hooking his finger under each x and tugging to add slack.

When he finished tying this one off he patted her hip. Her skirt meant there was no skin to skin contact, but the touch was far more intimate than when he'd been manipulating the corset. It was also a very Dom-y gesture.

Autumn took a deep breath, fighting through the hot flash of arousal that made her want to do something stupid. Something like turn around and straddle him, and grind her wet pussy against his cock as she kissed him, which would no doubt earn her a nice spanking.

Instead she walked back to her side of the table and sat. Her skirt rode up, and she was more than a little worried she would leave a wet spot on the leather seat when she stood again.

"Is that enough to allow you to eat?" Daniel asked.

Autumn picked up her plate and balanced it on her knees. "If I said it wasn't, would you loosen it more?"

"The lower half, certainly."

Daniel waited until she unrolled her silverware to pick up his own plate and balance it on his knee.

"But not the top?" She cut off a small bit of fish and put it in her mouth.

He finished chewing before responding. "No, I wouldn't. I will admit I selfishly want to enjoy the view while I eat."

Autumn laughed, aware her half-compressed boobs probably jiggled like jello.

They ate in silence, and while the silence wasn't exactly awkward, it wasn't comfortable. Autumn set aside her plate in favor of her wine glass and scooted so she could lean back against the edge of the sunken seating area. She watched him eat, which seemed strangely intimate. He glanced at her as he put a bite of steak into his mouth, then leaned back, still chewing.

He looked no less formal sans jacket. His shirt wasn't white the way she'd assumed, but actually more of a cream color. His tie was blue silk with a subtle stripe and his tie tack matched his cufflinks.

"I'm enjoying the view, too." She winked and tipped her glass towards him.

Daniel snorted out a laugh, then started to cough, having apparently half inhaled his food.

Autumn sat forward, legitimately alarmed, but he waved her away, covering his mouth with his napkin. After chugging half a glass of water, he set aside his plate and napkin.

His expression turned chiding and stern. Whoa. He did that disappointed authority figure look really well. For the first time in her life, Autumn had a burning desire to put on a little plaid skirt and play naughty schoolgirl.

That would be fun, but she also wanted to feel his arms wrap around her gently as he pulled her close. She wondered if she'd have an opportunity to run her fingers through his hair, to mess it up enough to make him look mussed. No, that was something a lover, not a play partner, did.

"Please don't make me choke," he said.

"Maybe it's all part of my evil plan."

"You have an evil plan? Hmm. Usually I'm the one with a kinky, evil plan."

He was fun. This was fun. Fun in a totally different way than the normal fun she had at Las Palmas.

"I make you laugh, you choke, and then I get to give you the Heimlich maneuver."

"Ma'am, are you planning to cop a feel?" He pressed his hand to his heart in mock moral outrage.

"It's either that or I spill some red wine on you so you have to take off your shirt." She pursed her lips and gave him a once over.

Daniel laughed, seemingly totally at ease with their conversation. With their flirty banter.

Shit.

She was flirting with him. Flirting was not a part of BDSM pre-scene negotiations. Flirting was for romance.

She had a rule. Never mix love and kink. It always ended badly.

"You have a devious mind, Autumn. I like it."

She managed a weak smile in response to his comment, but inside she was starting to panic.

She'd never had trouble following that rule at Las Palmas, at least in part because she always chose to scene with Doms she trusted and respected, but with whom she felt no desire to flirt.

Fuck. She was romantically attracted to him.

"Damn," she breathed. "I'm attracted to you."

Why had she just said that out loud?

He blinked several times, then leaned back and seemed to relax. "I cannot wait to hear the thought process that went into that statement, which your tone indicated you thought was a problem."

"Nope." Autumn shook her head. "Explaining would mean telling you some stuff about myself that, frankly, you have no right to know."

"We are about to be scene partners; that means that we need open lines of communication."

"It doesn't mean that I have to tell you all about my trust issues."

"A sub with trust issues." He leaned forward and picked up the wine bottle, tilting it towards her glass in question.

She held out her glass, let him pour her another. He topped up his own glass before sitting back.

Autumn patted her cleavage. "That's me. Sub with trust issues. Please tell me you have control issues."

His shoulders tightened, and he looked away. He took a sip

of wine before facing her again, smiling, though the skin around his eyes was tight. "Massive control issues."

"Excellent. For a second there I was worried we wouldn't be enough of a stereotype."

"Dodged that bullet." He lifted his glass towards her in a toast.

Autumn took a sip, lips twitching in amusement, her panic fading, though really it shouldn't have. Scening with him was a very bad idea.

They finished eating, conversation easy and just as flirty as before. She was having so much fun—though the word seemed inadequate—that when Daniel set down his glass and picked up the nearly forgotten envelope she was disappointed.

She didn't want this little dinner date to end.

She was such a fucking idiot.

Daniel took a thin stack of papers from the folder, turning the packet to show her the front page, which had her picture on it. "A copy of your checklist. Do you remember what you put?"

"I only joined last year, so I think so, but I should also say that I've learned a lot about what I will and won't do over the course of the year."

"Really?" He flipped a few pages. "Well, then it's a shame that you didn't update your list before the game."

"I would have, had I known the game was happening."

"Ah, but then there's no element of surprise."

"I don't like surprises. I doubt any member does. Lack of surprises is why we negotiate every moment of our scenes in advance."

"Is that what you do?" He set the papers on his lap, focus on her. "Negotiate every moment?"

"That's how it's supposed to be done."

"Come now, Autumn, you know there's no one right way to play."

"Don't presume to lecture me." For the first time real anger touched her words, and she could see from his body language that he was surprised by her calm, hard tone.

She looked away, taking a mental step back. The whole point of her membership here was to get away from the icy, risk-taking, disciplined person she was outside of here. When at Las Palmas she was supposed to be fun-loving Autumn, the person she'd been when she was younger, before bad relationships and a high stress job changed her. The sassy and dynamic version of herself that rarely saw the light of day anymore.

"Autumn."

His voice was low and rang with command. Stiffly, she returned her gaze to the man, the stranger, across from her. Flirting didn't make him any less a stranger, and she needed to remember that.

His gaze bore into hers, but his body was relaxed—a king totally in control, and confident on his throne. "I will presume to do far more to you than just lecture."

CHAPTER 3

Damn he was a lucky Dom. His partner was hot and sassy and how the *fuck* had he never seen her before?

Daniel watched Autumn's body language, loving the way her shoulders squared even as she uncrossed and then re-crossed her legs. She was the very picture of pissed off, but also aroused, submissive.

She'd taken him by surprise with the 'bat-shit' comment, and just kept surprising him, in the best possible ways.

The announcement of the checklist game had certainly shocked the hell out of him. Assigned partners, assigned letters, all because the club overseers thought they'd gotten complacent? He didn't need his sex life shaken up. BDSM was his outlet for a desperate, dark need for control. Anything that fucked with his ability to use BDSM as an outlet was risky.

The checklist game was wild and dramatic and he'd heard plenty of grumbling from among the Owners, Doms, and Masters who'd been standing near him during the all-club meeting.

He, it appeared, had gotten very lucky with Autumn.

They had chemistry. That had been apparent from the first words they exchanged, and he knew she felt it too.

Well, that was hardly some great insight on his part. Her *damn it, I'm attracted to you* comment made it pretty plain.

"You'll presume to do absolutely nothing without my consent." She notched her chin up in challenge.

"Of course not," he agreed.

She relaxed a little.

"Our letter is 'N' not 'R'," he teased, trying to get them back on their previous conversational footing.

"R? Wait, let me guess. Rape fantasy?"

"Yes." He tapped the papers.

"Well, 'n' could be for non-consent."

"You mean CNC?" Consensual non-consent was a more modern, and more current term than 'rape fantasy,' but the overseers were from an older generation of kinksters.

"You don't read much dark erotica do you?" She made an exaggerated sad face.

"No." He didn't bother to hide his grin. "I can't say I do."

"Well then, you're really missing out. Maybe I'll let you join my book club."

"You have a book club that reads non-consent dark erotica?"

"No, but I'm going to start one just so you can join," she assured him with mock solemnity.

Daniel let his head fall back and laughed. Damn, this was fun. Fun in a totally different way than the 'fun' he was used to having at Las Palmas. Fun wasn't something that had ever played a big part in his life.

When he finished laughing and glanced at her, the small smile she was struggling to hide was enchanting. Nearly as enchanting as the soft, bronzed mounds of her breasts plumped and lifted by her corset.

It had taken a fair amount of self control to stop himself

from spinning her around and burying his face in her cleavage after he'd finished adjusting her corset.

Needing something to do other than look at her pretty tits, Daniel picked up her checklist. It was already flipped to the page that had the items for the letter N on it.

The list of items for N was distressingly small and rather vanilla compared to some of what the other letters were going to deal with.

"We'll start with reviewing our checklist items, then we'll discuss," he declared.

"You already told me—it's nipple play, right?"

"Actually the phrase 'nipple play' isn't on here. We'll make that the implied fifth item. The first is actually 'name change'."

Autumn paused, the glass halfway to her mouth. "What?"

"That's actually what you put on the list." He tapped the page, where a bold hand had written *what?* next to "name change."

"You wrote 'what' with a question mark and then didn't actually check a box. The overseers said that for any unchecked or 'no comment' items, we could assume those were 'willing to try' or default to our own list."

For each item on the checklist there were four possible responses—"yes", "no", and "willing to try" were available options for each item on the list. The fourth response was to not answer, as she'd essentially done with name change.

"That's an…odd one." She rolled her wine glass against her lower lip. "I guess you could call me 'Fall' or something."

"You think you would get to choose the name change?" He sank a little steel into the words.

She stiffened, as he'd expected. He'd never had a sub be simultaneously easygoing and defensive. An odd, but compelling, combination for a submissive.

Though he was hardly a typical member of Las Palmas.

Daniel pushed those thoughts away. "The other three items

are all nipple related. Nipple clamps, nipple piercing, and nipple weights."

Autumn waved one hand dismissively. "We can knock this out in five minutes. My nipples are pierced, so we switch to rings, add weights, then remove both for a few minutes to use the clamps, and you can call me 'Fall' or 'Spring' or something."

"You're absolutely right."

She jerked a little in clear shock. She hadn't expected him to agree to that. And did she look a little disappointed? Maybe that was wishful thinking.

"You're right that we *could* do what you just outlined. We'd be the first pairing to start, and the first pairing to finish." He gestured around the still empty dining room.

He hadn't been the first person to receive his assignment packet, but he'd been the first person to walk out of the Conclave in search of his sub. He'd been planning to go the Den and use the intercom system to call for Autumn to meet him somewhere else in the club.

But he'd walked faster than planned, and caught up with the subs. The very sexy woman in the red corset with glossy gold-streaked dark hair had drawn his attention immediately. When she'd turned her head to the side, he'd recognized her from the picture he'd received.

"However, we're not going to," he finished.

"Oh?"

"Your idea would satisfy the technical requirements, but not the spirit, of the game."

"And what do you think the spirit of the game requires?"

His blood heated at the slight tremble in her words, in the way she was once more shifting restlessly. He wanted to see her let go, to hear her moaning in pleasure and sighing in emotional release.

Wanted her to give him control.

"You're going to submit to me. You're going to trust me

enough to do that. You're going to give me control of your body, and let me take care of you."

"Take care of me?" She shook her head, strands of hair whipping her face. "You mean—"

"I mean take care of you. Of your needs," he clarified.

"And your own." There was a bit of snark in her tone.

He let it go. For now.

"Yes. This arrangement is mutually beneficial."

She turned her head away, and he could see the tendons in her neck flexing. She was tense, tightly strung.

"Are you a switch?" he asked after a moment. He hadn't had a chance to go through every page of her paperwork, so maybe he'd missed something.

"I'd be a good Domme."

"That wasn't what I asked."

"It wasn't, was it?"

She still wasn't looking at him, and Daniel had a feeling that he wouldn't get any more answers, any real answers, unless he asked his questions as part of the scene, when she was feeling her submission.

He stood and walked around to where she sat. He'd deliberately chosen to approach her from her blind side, so she was looking away from him, and would have to turn her head to see him.

She stubbornly kept her head turned away, even when he was so close to her that the crease of his pants brushed her bare knee. Daniel hooked a lock of hair around his finger, twirling it idly. Standing while she was seated meant he had a lovely overhead view of her breasts rising and falling with her now rapid but uneven breaths.

He released the lock of hair so that it fell forward over her shoulder, the ends brushing the top of her breast.

"Autumn," he murmured.

"I don't even know you. You're a stranger," she snapped. The hard words were at odds with her breathing, with the way her body was softening as she leaned into him.

"Yes, I am," he agreed mildly.

"I would be crazy to agree to…"

"To submit to me."

She pressed her lips together so tightly that they almost disappeared. But her breath hitched, and when she exhaled it was almost a moan.

"But you're going to. Because you need to submit right now, don't you? And the game means that you either submit to me, or you walk away."

"Damn it," she whispered. "Damn it."

"I'm guessing that normally you play with Doms you've gotten to know over the course of time."

"Yes."

"You negotiate—how did you put it?—every moment of a scene."

"Not always." She sounded less sure.

"If playing with a partner you just met is one of your hard limits, then that is a different issue."

"It's not." Her breasts heaved as she took a heavy breath. "I mean of course there are times when I come to the club and just…" She raised one shoulder, let it fall.

Daniel cupped the back of her head in his hand, spearing his fingertips through her hair and massaging her scalp.

"Sometimes you scene with a stranger, a new partner, because your need outweighs your trust issues."

That got a small laugh out of her.

"Then," he continued, "tonight will be one of those nights."

She reacted to the words with a slight catch to her breath.

"You're going to submit to me," he murmured.

"I shouldn't."

He kept up the scalp massage until she tipped her head back, letting the weight of her skull fall into his hand. Her eyes were closed, her breathing slow and even. Her legs had relaxed, one now leaning fully against his knee, her thighs parted just enough that if he'd wanted to, he could have slid his hand between her thighs and touched her pussy.

"Why?" he murmured low and gentle. "Why shouldn't you?"

"Because I'm attracted to you."

Ah ha. They'd circled around. To a topic he found all too interesting. "And why does that matter?"

"Because I care what—"

He heard her teeth click together as her eyes flew open. She'd stopped herself from finishing that sentence, and as she looked up at him, her eyes wide as if shocked by her own near-admission, he knew she was about to close down.

Unless he did something to prevent it.

Daniel shifted, each movement sure and precise, because for the last several minutes he'd been planning how he'd touch her next.

He pivoted, sliding one foot between hers. His leg forced her knees apart. He braced his knee against the front of the bench as he tightened the hand tangled in her hair. He brought his other hand up and curled it loosely around her neck.

Autumn gasped and raised her hands to grip his wrist. But she didn't try to tug his hand away.

Pinned in place as he stood over her, controlling her like this made Daniel's dominant side rise. Dark needs slithered through him, whispering of all the delicious things he could do to her.

"Autumn, what is your safe word?"

"Pickle. My slowdown word is onion."

"I don't use a stoplight style system." Some people chose to use the words red, yellow, and green as a safe word system. Yellow meant the sub needed to pause the scene, while "red" functioned as the traditional safe word which stopped the scene all together.

"If something is bothering you, if you need me to stop or

slow down, tell me. I will always listen, I promise you that. I want open, honest, non-coded communication."

She actually relaxed, her hands falling away from his wrist. "So if I say 'oh no, your dick is just far too big, stop' you'll take it literally?"

Daniel let out a startled laugh. He adjusted his hands, so he was cupping her head between his palms, thumbs just in front of her ears, fingers sunk into all that lovely soft hair.

"Oh I most definitely would stop," he assured her. "I'd stop touching you, playing with you, pleasuring you..."

"That's diabolical," she whispered.

"A little sadism in a Dom is a good thing." And then, just because he knew she'd appreciate the comment, said, "And a little sadism never hurt anyone."

She let out another peal of laughter.

He leaned down, close enough that he could have kissed her. He didn't, but he could have.

"Autumn, you mentioned my dick."

"Yes, yes I did."

"But we will not be having sex."

"Of course not. A BDSM scene doesn't mean sex."

"Doesn't always mean sex," he corrected.

"We just met," she said in what should have been agreement, but sounded a little unsure. Dare he say, disappointed.

"Yes." He dropped his hands and straightened. "So why were you thinking about my dick?"

"I like to objectify men like that." Her response was too quick.

"I think it has something to do with you finding me attractive."

"Need your ego stroked so bad you keep bringing it up?"

He wanted to push her, but she'd folded her arms across her waist, her shoulders hunched defensively.

Daniel put one finger under her chin, tipping her face up.

"Are you ready?" he asked solemnly.

She relaxed, and he was fairly sure that was due to him backing the conversation away from an uncomfortable topic.

"Yes."

"Master Daniel," he corrected. "Or Sir."

She stiffened, just slightly, then said, "Yes, Master Daniel."

He moved back, making space for her to stand, then offered her his hand.

Autumn placed her fingers in his, let him pull her to her feet.

Daniel ran his thumb across her palm. Her eyes fluttered closed for a moment, and when she opened them they seemed darker and softer than they had been a moment ago.

She was…perfect.

The word came to mind unbidden, followed quickly by a rush of desire so strong that he felt it in his gut. He wanted *her*. This woman in particular. It wasn't always like that. He came here knowing he could exorcise his own demon by topping a willing sub. It was a safe outlet for his needs.

And while no two subs were the same, and he always made sure that the scene served both their needs, his desire was usually for the scene, not for a particular sub.

But he wanted her.

Wanted to kiss her.

Sit her on his lap so he could feed her with one hand while the other played with her nipples.

Cuddle her in aftercare, and then walk her to her car when they were done.

Most of all, he wanted to fuck her.

He'd stricken that particular activity from the scene, and now that he'd said it, going back on his word would make him the kind of irresponsible, self-control-less asshole who wasn't fit to be a Dom.

No fucking.

Damn it.

CHAPTER 4

This is a scene, not a date.
He is your play partner, not your date.
You can sub for him, you can't date him.

As mantras went, it was a little repetitive, but functional.

Or maybe the fact that Daniel was now undeniably in his mental top space—the other side of the sub-space coin—was doing more to keep her from feeling defensive than her mantra was.

If this had been a date… well.

Intimate relationships were kept in two completely separate buckets. The dating and falling in love bucket was kept very far away from the D/s bucket. The contents were never allowed to mix.

Usually, it wasn't a problem, and past heartbreak and trauma was a good motivator for the separation.

For the first time since becoming a member of Las Palmas, Autumn was having trouble.

Daniel was the kind of man she could date and fall in love with. She wanted to plop him into the relationship bucket.

He was also the kind of man she would *never* allow herself to fall in love with. He belonged firmly in the D/s bucket.

Because he was a Dom.

Because he knew she was a sub.

And once a man knew she was a sexual submissive they wouldn't respect her. They'd use her desire to submit against her. They wouldn't love her; they'd either think she was too needy and not worth the extra work. Or think they owned her.

You know that's not right. You know that's fear and pain talking. Also, you're a horrible hypocrite.

Autumn forced her internal monologue to shut up as she and Daniel stepped into one of the club's elegant inner courtyards.

The *Sub Rosa* court was elegant and discreet in comparison to the others. The canopy of hybrid desert climbing roses sheltered the outdoor space, and added a romantic feel that could provide a delicious counterpoint to the kinky and perverse activities that took place in the courtyard itself or one of the surrounding playrooms.

A platform in the center provided a stage where scenes could be performed, or subs put on display. The rest of the courtyard had plush outdoor furniture arranged in conversational groupings, or lone chairs or couches surrounded by heavy wine-barrel pots with lattice panels of climbing roses where a couple could have the illusion of privacy.

Daniel led her to a wide, armless chair sheltered on two sides by pots of roses and climbing vines.

The club had started to come alive, people in fetwear walking around with a bemused, unsure air which was unusual and most likely thanks to the game.

Daniel took a seat, draping his suit jacket over the back of the couch. His gaze raked her, and this time it wasn't just appreciative, but possessive.

It's not a date. It's a D/s scene.

The way he was looking at her was most definitely Dom-like

rather than date-like. If a date looked at her like that, she would be reaching for her pepper spray and making wide eyes at the server as a warning that she might need help with an escape plan.

"What are you thinking about?" Daniel asked, surprising her.

"Context," she answered honestly.

His eyebrows rose in question.

"The way you're looking at me would be...scary if we were on a date."

"This isn't a date."

Autumn flinched, as if...well not as if he'd hit her, because her reaction to impact play wasn't to flinch—it was to wiggle and moan. She flinched as if his words had slid straight into the soft, dark core of her fears.

Of course this wasn't a date. She'd made it complicated because she was attracted to him.

Maybe some stupid part of her still thought she could have it both ways, even though bitter experience had taught her that wasn't true.

In some alternate universe they met at a bar, had the same chemistry and banter, and that led to a relationship and eventually falling in love.

A relationship where she'd be sexually unfulfilled because she'd never admit to needing to be sexually dominated.

He'd met her at the club. He knew she was a submissive. That should have made it so easy for her to keep from thinking of him as anything but a play partner.

She swallowed back the hot embarrassment that was the most prevalent of the emotions running through her. She stared at one of the pale pink roses on the vine to her left and told herself to pull it together. It was hardly as if she were about to undergo something traumatic. She'd embarrassed herself by using the word 'date.' She needed to get her head in the game.

A very attractive, dominant man was going to play with her breasts.

Arousal slid through her and she focused on that. Desire and submissive need could mute other nasty thoughts. Add in D/s, and that desire and need became all-consuming.

"Out of curiosity, how is it that I'm looking at you?" Daniel asked. There was maybe a hint of worry in his voice.

"Like a Dom."

His lips twitched and he seemed to relax. "I'm not sure if that's disappointingly predictable, or…"

No, no. Don't tease me, not in the witty banter way. I need you to be all Dom so I don't start thinking about dating again.

When she didn't respond Daniel sat forward, his elbows on his knees.

"We seem to have a problem." His voice had deepened and had an edge to it.

Her skin prickled and her ass clenched.

"You think I sound like a Dom, but you aren't sounding particularly submissive."

Before she could reply, Daniel was on his feet. He stepped into her personal space, one hand gripping her waist, the other tangling in her hair.

"Look at me, Autumn." He paired the words with using his hold on her hair to force her to look at him.

She could have closed her eyes, but it wouldn't have been submission, it would have been hiding.

Damn it, his eyes were a beautiful blue-gray up close, with maybe even a little hint of brown around the outer rim.

"Our scene starts when I sit back down. I'm giving you a few more minutes, only because I know this is an unusual set of circumstances for starting a scene."

"I understand."

"You called me Master Daniel before. Let's hear it again."

"Master Daniel."

"Do you need me to help you get into your submissive mindset?"

Normally, she didn't need that, but with him...

"Maybe. I'm sorry, it's just that I..."

He waited, but when she didn't say anything else he shook his head. "You're going to finish that sentence for me, but not right now."

He released her hair for a moment, reaching back for his jacket. He carelessly tossed it onto the ground, then cupped her head once more, fingers buried in her hair.

"You're going to kneel for me. You're going to spread your knees, and if you aren't wearing any panties, I'll get my first good look at your pussy."

"You're going to hold that position. Kneeling, head down, legs spread, until I give you permission to move. If you disobey, you'll get a spanking. Not a fun spanking. You won't be over my lap. I'll bend you over this chair and it will hurt."

Autumn blew out a low, slow breath, all thoughts of dating pushed down and buried under his words and touch.

He leaned in, cheek brushing hers as he whispered, "I might decide to spank you either way. But if you're a good girl, you'll enjoy the spanking much more."

He released her, inching back enough that there was space between them.

"If you're not comfortable submitting to me, there is no shame in that. If you want to walk away, even if it's just for tonight, this weekend, there is no shame in that, either."

He let the words hang in the air. It was meant to give her a chance to turn away, but all it did was tighten the tension that gripped her.

The corset, despite having been loosened, felt too tight. She was hyper aware of her nipples inside the corset, and of the wetness between her legs, which had doubtless soaked the fabric of the black satin thong.

The air around them was still and heavy. The warmth from a nearby heat lamp seemed too hot against her arousal-sensitized skin.

Daniel lowered himself to the wide chair, leaning back and stretching his arms along the back. It pulled the fabric of his shirt tight against his arms and pecs.

The scene had begun.

She hung there, unsure. Unsure of what she should do, but also of what she was feeling. He wiped away that doubt and gave her something to focus on with a single command.

"Kneel."

CHAPTER 5

The skirt finally gave up when Daniel toed her knees another inch further apart. By her calculation, she'd been kneeling here for *hours*. In strictly linear time it was probably closer to twenty minutes, but time passed differently in BDSM play. So far, she'd managed to mostly keep her skirt in place by sandwiching the fabric between her heels and ass.

When she obediently spread her knees in response to the nudge from his toe, the stretchy fabric of the bandage-style skirt rolled up, forming a black band of fabric at the bottom of her corset.

She shivered, both because cold air now hit skin that had been covered a moment ago, and because she was that much closer to being naked. Kneeling before him like this had allowed her to sink into her submission.

Autumn wanted to be naked for him.

It was miserable and frustrating and perversely arousing kneeling for him, with only a few layers of fabric between her knees and the sandy soil of the courtyard. Even more frustrating, she had her back to the stage in the center of the courtyard, where a scene was currently taking place. She could hear

35

the thud and slap of impact play, the deep murmur of a Dom talking his sub through a scene, and the sighs and cries of the sub in question. She could hear it all, but couldn't see anything.

After telling her to kneel, Daniel hadn't said anything else, instead using all non-verbal commands. When she'd twisted to look at the stage, he'd grasped her chin, turned her to face him, then put a hand on her head and forced it down. When she dug her nails into her thighs, restless and seeking stimulation, he'd reached down and grabbed her wrists, forcing her to flip her hands so they were palm up.

And finally, he'd started nudging her knee apart with the toe of his shoe.

Behind her, a woman moaned, "No. It hurts. Please… Harder."

Autumn bit the side of her tongue, imagining what was happening to the woman. Maybe a thick plug was being forced into her ass. Or clamps placed on her nipples and slowly tightened.

She wanted that pain. Wanted him to start with her. To touch her and hurt her and help her find the sweet release she needed.

If someone was getting nipple weights or clamps it should be her, damn it.

And yet…being forced to wait didn't dampen her arousal. Forced to kneel with nothing to look at but his feet and her own spread legs was exactly the kind of frustration she enjoyed.

This slow, silent, but powerful start to their scene meant that when he reached down and placed a single finger under her chin, tilting her face up, she was soft and willing, letting him raise her face while she kept her eyes submissively lowered.

She sensed his focus and attention as he inspected her face, her body.

"Gorgeous." His finger slid down the line of her throat, and then kept going.

She caught her breath as he traced the plump mounds of her breasts where they were exposed above the top of her corset.

"Kneel up."

She raised her butt off her heels, her feet a little tingly because she'd partially lost feeling in them thanks to how she'd been sitting. When she swayed, his hands came out to cup her ribs, offering her an anchor point.

It was done without comment, and showed that he was paying very close attention to her, even if he was, ostensibly, focused on watching the scene behind her. She leaned into his hands for a moment, sighing in pleasure.

His thumbs swept across the front of the corset, and she hated that she couldn't feel that touch as anything more than a little pressure.

"I've allowed you to keep your breasts hidden from me for too long," he murmured.

"I'm sorry, Sir."

"What are you sorry for? I want to hear it."

"I'm sorry that my breasts are hidden from you."

"Stand up and take off the corset."

He kept one hand on her, but offered her the other, palm up, to brace herself on as she stood. She'd kicked off her shoes when she first knelt. The material of his suit jacket was warm and soft under her feet as she found her balance, regretting that his hand dropped away from her as soon as she did.

When she took a breath she smelled the very faint scent of roses, a more wild, green scent than came from hothouse cultivated roses. She also smelled leather conditioner, and the faint trace of a feminine perfume.

"Strip," Daniel commanded, his voice now hard.

Autumn softened at the command in his words, then reached for the bottom of her corset. Re-lacing a corset every time it had to be put on was madness, so this one, like most corsets, had hidden hook and eye closures running down the front. Getting dressed at the club involved loosening the corset lacings, wrapping it around herself and fastening the front closures, then having another sub tighten it at the back.

Pinching the bottom edges, she squeezed them towards each other and undid the first few hook and eye closures. She planned to work from the bottom up, but Daniel stopped her.

"No. Start at the top. I want to see your breasts trying to escape the corset."

Autumn glanced at him from under her lashes, and slid her hands up her torso. She cupped her breasts, fingertips digging into the exposed and plumped mounds above the top edge of her corset.

Daniel's lips twitched into a smile, but he shook his head in a wordless rebuke.

She shifted her weight, her damp labia sliding against one another. Shoving her thumbs down under the top edge of her corset, she pinched the fabric and squeezed the panels together, momentarily compressing her breasts even more. For one delicious second she could barely breathe it was so tight, and rather than frightening, she found that moment exhilarating.

Then the first few hooks were open, and when she inhaled, her breasts forced the top edges of the corset apart, exposing the inner curve of her pressed-together breasts.

Impatient now, she kept going, unfastening the corset with more haste than grace. When the final hook was undone she paused, holding the corset closed as she looked at Daniel through her lashes.

He sat forward, focused and intense, then pointed at the ground with a sharp, commanding gesture.

She dropped the corset.

Her areolae tightened as the cold air hit them, and as she took a breath, the slim silver bars with their rhinestone ball ends caught the light. She had thinner than normal jewelry, because she didn't want the piercings to show through her bra, but also didn't want to have to wear a thickly padded bra.

And she liked the aesthetic of dainty jewelry. In her mind, nipples deserved to be adorned with delicate beauty. Not that she didn't occasionally use thicker bars, especially if she was wearing nipple shields that required a heavier, longer bar in order to stay in place.

She took another deep breath, watching him watch her breasts rise and fall.

"Get rid of the skirt," he commanded.

She wiggled the roll of fabric down and off. Though it hadn't been covering more than a one-inch band of skin around her waist, removing it made her feel more exposed. She was naked except for the black thong, which was soaked from her own arousal, and felt like it was stuck to her labia.

"You have lovely breasts." Daniel sat back. "Hands on your head. I want to see them lifted."

Lacing her fingers together and resting them on the crown of her head, her breasts now raised and exposed, made her pussy clench with need. It was a little shocking how turned on she was given that he'd barely touched her. Usually it took more physical touch to get her to this point.

Maybe you're more turned on because this isn't just a scene. You're subbing for a man you like and are attracted to.

The thought, the words, made her flinch, and stole some of her pleasure. Embarrassment, and not the fun, sexy kind, took big bites out of her arousal.

"Cold?" Daniel had, apparently, noticed her shiver.

"A little," she murmured, focused on an internal battle not to fall out of the moment.

"A little what?" he asked.

She missed the warning note in his voice.

"A little cold," she replied, distracted by panicky thoughts about her attraction to him.

Daniel surged to his feet, his eyes hard and glittering even in the low light of the courtyard. Her own eyes widened as she realized what she'd just done.

He'd been prompting her to add a "Sir" onto that sentence. Not asking her to clarify what her "a little" comment had been in reference to.

Daniel gripped the back of her neck. The tip of his thumb and one finger pressed into the soft spots just under each ear.

He jerked her forward, and in a bid to cool his irritation by being extra submissive she kept her hands on her head, even as he used his hold on her neck to push her down so she was kneeling on the seat of the wide chair.

He forced her upper body forward, and when she tried to angle it so her upper chest and shoulders rested on the back of the chair, he jerked her further forward, so it was her waist that rested on the top of the chair, her upper body extended over the back, breasts dangling. Unable to keep her balance with her arms up, she unlaced her fingers and grabbed hold of the chair, elbows tucked in at her sides.

He released her neck. She took a deep breath, fighting the mingled alarm and excitement that coursed through her.

"I'm sorry, Master Daniel. I was thinking about something else."

He didn't reply.

She craned her neck to look at him where he stood beside the chaise, his expression mildly disappointed.

For most subs, that was probably a look men gave them only when they were in a scene. But for her that mild, almost disinterested expression triggered some bad memories. Memories that had nothing to do with this moment, and everything to do with her submission.

Shit, shit, shit.

She closed her eyes and tried to focus on what was going on around her. Let the ambient smells and sounds of the club remind her of where she was and what she could get from being here. It would have been better if she'd been able to see the scene on the stage, but right now all she could see was a massive pot filled with succulents, one of the posts around which the desert roses climbed, and the hard-packed sandy ground.

The sound of a belt being whipped off shocked her back into that needy, submissive place. She twisted in time to see Daniel folding his belt in half, the buckle and tail ends held in his fist, the needy fear of a punishment chasing away her ghosts.

"I'm sorry, Master Daniel."

"I'm sure you are. And I know you weren't looking for a punishment, were you? You weren't trying to be a brat." He stroked her ass with the belt, gentle caresses with smooth, slick leather.

"I wasn't, no. I don't play brat."

"I didn't think so. Which almost makes it worse."

She shifted a little, putting her hands under her stomach so she was resting on them rather than directly on the narrow wooden back. "You prefer brats?"

"No, that's not what I'm saying. You weren't paying attention. You weren't in the moment, and you should have been."

Autumn put the tip of her tongue between her teeth to stop herself from saying something that would not help the situation.

He came closer and crouched so he could see her face, and she could see his. His lips twitched. "Does it hurt? Holding back whatever sassy comment you clearly want to make."

"I said I wasn't a brat."

"Brat and sass are two distinctly different things."

That surprised her. "You think so?"

"I do. And anyone who doesn't is an idiot. Sassy comments can be done in a bratty way, but pure sassy is rarely also bratty."

"You're a connoisseur."

41

"I am. And if you'd said 'a little cold' in a different tone I might have thought it was brat. But you were distracted. Not in the moment." He stroked the side of one hanging breast with the back of his finger. "That is as much my fault as yours."

She never really considered the side of her breast a major erogenous zone. Nipple, of course. Underside? Yes.

Daniel had just proven she was too narrow minded. She felt that gentle stroke, his first time touching her bare breasts, in every part of her body.

"I'm paying attention now." She'd meant the comment to be dry. It came out breathless.

Daniel laughed as he stood, and it wasn't some menacing dark chuckle; it was a real, happy laugh that made her own lips twitch.

And made her heart race a little because she really liked this guy. If this had been a date—

The first slap of his belt against her ass shocked more than it hurt. She jumped, glad she had her hands under her to protect her middle.

"I lost you again there for a moment, didn't I?"

Slap.

This one was firmer, but still just a quick sting. His belt wasn't an impact toy, and so he wasn't really using it as one.

"Yes, Sir," she whispered. She wasn't normally a whisperer, but her throat was tight and it was the best she could manage.

"Something is going on in your head that's distracting you."

Air whistled this time before the belt landed again.

Autumn whimpered and her pussy pulsed. She enjoyed impact play for impact play's sake. She was rarely "punished" unless that was part of the negotiated scene, and usually she agreed to it because it was part of the Dom's needs. She'd take a plug up her ass then go over a man's lap for a spanking with a smile on her face, because she enjoyed the physical sensations, not because she got off on the taboo idea of being spanked.

What Daniel was doing right now was…different. He was punishing her for not paying attention. Not being present.

The first time when she failed to add a 'Sir' or 'Master Daniel' onto the end of the sentence, even after he'd warned her, it had been obvious she wasn't really paying attention.

This second time, when she'd been distracted thinking about dating him, he'd noticed even though it hadn't been as obvious. That meant he'd accurately read her body language and facial expression, which indicated that while *she* might not have been paying attention, *he* had been watching her closely.

"When was the last time you were whipped with a belt?"

"It's been…a while. Usually we just—" She sucked in breath as he landed another strike. "—uh, use impact play implements."

"No improvised punishments." It wasn't a question but a statement. "Three more."

Slap.

Slap.

Slap.

The final blows fell in quick sensation, landing with a popping, stinging intensity. They weren't really that hard, which was appropriate since she wasn't warmed up, but they weren't just for show either. She could feel the spots where the belt had landed, though she doubted the pink marks would last more than a few minutes.

He'd spanked her, hurt her in a small but important way.

She welcomed the pain. Hopefully it would cement in her mind that Daniel was a Dom, and her play partner. That their chemistry didn't matter. That it was already too late, no matter how much she might like him, because he knew she was a submissive.

His belt buckle clinked as he tossed it down, as casually careless with it as he had been with his coat.

Then he was gripping her shoulders, helping her straighten

up. At some point during the spanking her eyes had drifted closed. By the time she blinked them open, he was gone, circling around behind her.

"May I touch your ass?"

"You're asking permission? You didn't ask before you whipped off that belt." She was kneeling on the chair, back straight, hands braced on the back.

"No, but I knew from your checklist that impact play is important to you, and punishment is, well, it's standard practice. But impact play doesn't automatically mean intimate touching. Our checklist items mean I will be touching your breasts, but there is no need for me to touch your ass with my hands if you would rather I not."

"Anyone not in the lifestyle would find that statement, and your question in general, ludicrous."

"Poor vanilla bastards," Daniel said fervently.

She giggled—ugh, giggled—then cleared her throat and said, "Yes, you may touch me, Sir."

His fingers were cool as they danced over her skin. Autumn sucked in a breath and her glutes clenched. He palmed her ass, one cheek in each hand, then leaned in close. Close enough she could feel his body heat on her back, and feel his breath moving her hair when he exhaled.

He gave her ass a little squeeze and she pushed her hips back, pressing her butt into his hands.

He squeezed again, fingers digging into her in a way that was anything but casual. She braced the heels of her hands on the back of the chair and pushed back far enough that her ass touched his body. She ground against him. His cock was hard; she could feel it through his pants, and that just turned her on more.

She wanted him to undo his pants, slide his cock deep into her pussy, and take her. She wanted his cock in her while he bit her neck and pinched her nipples. Wanted him to fuck her so hard and so good that all she could do was hold on to the chair, brace herself against the onslaught of pleasure his fucking would bring.

Daniel's hands slid to her ribs and he jerked her up, her bare back against his clothed chest. He ground his cock against her ass, chin rubbing against her hair as he leaned in to whisper in her ear.

"What a good little slutty submissive you are. I bet you'll do anything if I promise to fuck you. If you're obedient I might be willing to let you have my cock tomorrow, but we'll have to negotiate it. So keep being a submissive slut, and—"

The words were like a bucket of ice water to the face. Shocking. Cold.

Painful.

Every muscle in her body went taut and tears tightened her throat.

Slut.

Submissive slut.

Good girl.

Words she hated. Words that made her feel stupid. Words that made her hate herself. And hate the person who said them.

The words were bad enough, but the worst of it was his *tone*.

This wasn't the way he'd talked to her at dinner. Wasn't even the calm, commanding tone he'd used to give her orders. This was the sneering, derisive tone of a man who didn't respect the woman he was with. Who thought…no, *knew*, she was less than because of what she wanted. Because she both enjoyed sex and was a submissive

It hurt. A barely healed scar was ripped open, the pain familiar but no less heartbreaking for the familiarity.

Coming from Daniel, the man she'd flirted with and who knew the difference between sassy and bratty…it hurt worse.

Autumn pushed back, using her bodyweight to throw him off balance so he took a few steps back. She was already moving, whirling off the bench and stooping to grab something to cover herself.

Her corset lay in a heap, and there was no point in trying to get it back on, so she snatched up his jacket, holding it to her chest as she retreated, backing away from their little spot and into an open area of the courtyard. There were now plenty of other people in the courtyard, but she ignored them.

She was shaking, teeth nearly chattering, so she clenched her jaw and finally looked up. Looked at him.

Daniel stood in the shadows, his eyes wide, his hands loose at his sides. He opened his mouth, but didn't say anything. He looked utterly confused. Or maybe that was her wishful thinking, and that look was really disappointment, disgust, not confusion.

"Autumn..."

The sound of her name on his lips, the way he was looking at her... It was too much.

Autumn turned and walked away.

CHAPTER 6

What the fuck had just happened? Scenes went sideways. It happened to even the most experienced players.

Daniel wouldn't consider himself an expert, but he was far from inexperienced. Usually, if a scene had to be stopped, or started deviating from plan, he could sense the issue coming, and knew how to get himself and his partner reengaged and back on track. That focus was a major part of his need for control. A need he only released when he was Master Daniel.

This time he had no idea what had gone wrong.

He stood, stupefied, as Autumn hurried away. She wasn't running, but it was a quick walk.

Her naked back—naked save for the thin strings of her thong underwear and the already fading pink marks from the belt—disappeared into the shadowed hallway that surrounded the courtyard.

More than a few heads had turned to watch her, then track back to him. Some Doms and Masters who'd noticed her retreat hit him with hard stares.

That shocked him into moving, because if he didn't do something, one of the men giving him the gimlet eye might take it upon themselves to go check on Autumn.

But Autumn was *his*.

He snatched up his belt and started feeding it through the loops as he hurried after her. She had given him control so he could satisfy her need, both their needs. This situation had just spiraled out of his control and grim determination, a need to make it right, to understand and fix it, made every muscle in his body tight.

He had long legs, and they ate up the ground, closing the distance she'd put between them.

He caught up to her on the path between the Sub Rosa court and the next building over. The covered flagstone path was lit only by the starlight that peeked through the slatted cover overhead, and ambient light filtering out of the Sub Rosa court.

He didn't touch her, that was inappropriate bordering on unacceptable, but he slid past her, took a few steps, turned, and stopped, blocking her path. She pulled up short, but didn't look at him.

"We need to talk," he said softly, his tone gentle when inside he felt hard and ragged. "It would be remiss of me to let you leave right now. At the very least you need aftercare."

"We didn't scene."

"We did," he countered.

She hugged herself, wrinkling the fabric of his jacket with her tight, desperate hold. "I..."

That was all she said. Daniel gave her another minute, but when she didn't speak, his Dom side took over.

"We'll talk in private." He stepped sideways off the path, between two of the columns that supported the pergola-like path cover. The rocky soil, loose rather than hard packed as it was in the courtyards, crunched under his shoes. He looked down at her bare feet, then back at her.

"If you wait a moment I'll go get your shoes."

It was a risk. The moment he was gone she'd probably disappear into the Sub Rosa court.

To his surprise she joined him, walking out of the striped shadows and into the silvery light cast down by moon and stars.

"You deserve aftercare too," she said softly. "And you're right, what we did was enough to…"

Her words ended with a heavy sigh.

Without touching her, Daniel guided her onto the grounds of the estate, and around the corner of the Sub Rosa court building.

The manicured lawns—which he was fairly certain were fake grass due to California's perpetual water shortage—started at the edge of the building and extended over large swaths of the grounds. From here they could see the Conclave, the edge of the Iron Court, and even the tops of a few cars in the parking lot at the front of the property. No one would come this way. They had total privacy.

Daniel took off his tie and tie tack, ignoring the way she tensed, and stuffed it into his pocket. With quick, economical movements he unbuttoned and slipped off his dress shirt, laying it on the ground beside the wall.

Autumn looked at it, then at him.

"Won't you get cold?"

"I'll be fine." His undershirt was thin cotton, but he was still far from naked. "I'm more worried about you."

Autumn turned her back to him and then slipped his jacket on rather than just holding it up. The sleeves hid her hands and it covered her butt. She turned to face him, and he had to quickly school his features.

The jacket was big enough around the waist to overlap, but while he was roughly the same circumference from waist to chest, she was most definitely not, and the jacket gaped, showing off the inner curves of her breasts, which were

49

plumped like an offering because she'd crossed her arms below them.

They both took a minute to stare at her moonlit cleavage.

"At least my nipples are covered," she pointed out.

"Yes, good thing, because looking at your cold, tight nipples would be…" There wasn't very much acting involved in letting his voice trail off into a groan.

She grinned at him, and something inside him relaxed. She wasn't upset anymore. They could talk to one another. That meant he would understand her, and what had gone wrong.

She turned and sat on his shirt, leaning her back against the wall. He dropped down beside her, shivering at the touch of the cold plaster against his back. Stretching his legs out, his glossy shoes an odd contrast to her dusty toes, he settled in to wait.

The silence stretched, but it wasn't awkward, at least for him. He was happy to wait. He wasn't sure he would have been this patient with another partner. Something about her was different. Maybe it was because of the game, because the decision to play together had been made for them.

It had been natural and effortless, slipping from conversation to scene. She'd effectively run from him, but it didn't feel like manipulation.

She hadn't used her safe word.

For some that would be evidence that she wasn't really upset, but instead being deliberately bratty or trying to manipulate the scene.

He knew, with a certainty that had no basis in fact or evidence, that there was another explanation.

They sat there long enough that the goosebumps on his arms were starting to feel permanent when she finally sighed, drawing her knees up, hands curled around her shins.

"I'm sorry."

"You have no reason to be sorry. You didn't do anything wrong," he assured her. And he meant it. He was in control of the scene, and that meant anything that happened was his responsibility.

"You're only saying that because I haven't confessed."

"Confession is good for the soul." He couldn't stop the disdain that tainted his words, but hoped she could tell it was for the phrase, not her.

"And spankings are good for people's emotional health." She turned to look at him. "That wasn't sarcasm, by the way. Getting spanked until I cry always makes me feel better."

A cold, dark realization gripped him, and Daniel bent one knee under so he could twist and face her. "Autumn, if having a belt used brought up past trauma—"

"No, no. It wasn't that."

The sick feeling in his stomach subsided. He sometimes forgot that for normal people, having a parent use a belt for punishment was severe. That hadn't been his experience. A belt would have been a relief.

He let his head drop. "Thank the universe. I looked over your list and thought belts were okay, but if I overlooked something…"

"No, in this scenario I'm not the victim. I'm the asshole."

Daniel had no idea what to say to that, so he stayed silent.

She tipped her head back, looking up at the stars. "I probably seem nuts, don't I?"

"No. You seem, you *are*, lovely and quick-witted."

"Our witty banter is part of the problem," she murmured.

He prided himself on being able to understand people, particularly submissives. A solid understanding of who a sub was and what they needed—sometimes that understanding even eclipsing what they were willing to acknowledge of their own needs—allowed him to truly and fully take control in the power exchange. Right now…he was lost.

"Autumn, I hate to say this…but I have no fucking clue what you're thinking or feeling. What you need."

"I know. I'm sorry."

"I'll tell you what I do know, instead." He tapped his hand against his knee, gathering his thoughts. "You didn't run in order to manipulate me or the scene. You aren't a brat." He stopped to consider. "I don't think you tried to initiate a primal play chase either."

She nodded.

"Those are the things that aren't happening. But what *is* happening... I'd love for you to tell me, when you're ready."

"Can I ask an odd question, first?"

"Of course."

She looked pale in the moonlight, almost ethereal, though the aesthetic was spoiled by the too-large suit jacket. "I want to ask you what you think would have happened if we'd met at a bar."

The question caught him completely off guard. He stared into the middle distance, thinking. What would have happened? He would have noticed her, he was sure of that. Would he have asked if he could buy her a drink? He didn't know. Not that he wouldn't have wanted to, but his past made it difficult for him to imagine himself in romantic relationships. He'd had them—it had actually been a girlfriend in his grad school years who'd introduced him to D/s, laying the groundwork for what would become his control outlet.

"Would it have been a meet-cute moment?" she went on. "I buy you a drink, you come over to say thank you, maybe make a cute comment about how usually you're the one to buy the drinks."

She pressed her lips together, and though he wanted to comment, he stayed quiet, sensing that she needed to get through this without being interrupted.

"But I'm not going to ask that, because that wouldn't really be fair, would it? Maybe you're married or seeing someone and coming here is part of your open relationship. If that's the case, you don't talk to strange women in bars."

"I'm not married, or in a romantic relationship," he said quietly.

"Oh." She glanced at him, then away. "I guess my point is that in this imaginary situation where we were both out at the bar because we were single and ready to mingle…"

She turned her face, laying her cheek on her knee so she was huddled into a tight ball. Her face was half in shadow, her nose, chin, and lower lip gilded by silvery light.

"…I would have bought you a drink, or let you buy me one. We would have spent the night talking. You have to admit our banter was immediately on-point."

"No argument here. We have chemistry."

She winced and though he didn't know what about that comment had hurt her, he wished he hadn't spoken.

"Yeah…and that's the problem. I'm attracted to you, and not just like a sub who thinks she's met a Dom she can scene well with. I like you. I'd want to date you, if we had met at that imaginary bar."

Daniel made sure his surprise didn't show. The last thing he wanted was to hurt her feelings, and he was sure acting surprised would do exactly that.

And honestly, what she said wasn't surprising. Everything she said was true. They had good chemistry, their conversations had flowed easily since the first word. She was funny, sexy, and gorgeous. She was probably smart and successful too, if she was a member of Las Palmas.

It wasn't what she'd said that was surprising, but the fact that she'd said it at all.

There was an unspoken rule that members didn't use the club as a dating pool. This wasn't a place to come and find a like-minded individual in order to form a long term relationship.

It happened, but due to organic formation of relationships, not because someone set out to deliberately find a romantic partner.

The other side of that was that if a member married or began a serious relationship, how they planned to explain their membership to their partner had to be disclosed to the overseers. And if two married members got divorced, well...he'd heard the stories about Master Hadrian and Cleo's divorce, though he'd never met Hadrian.

"Autumn, are you saying...you want to go on a date before we scene?" He understood what she was saying, but so far nothing she'd said explained why she'd reacted the way she had.

Autumn took a breath and sat up, staring out across the grounds rather than looking at him. "The men I date don't know I'm a sexual submissive."

"You haven't dated anyone for long enough that you're comfortable telling them?"

"It's not a time issue. I was with someone, someone I'd been dating for a year and a half when I first joined. We broke up not long after, but for a while I was doing both—scening here on the weekends, and still dating him during the week."

"You didn't think he'd be interested in any sort of kink or D/s?" Daniel frowned. "Or were you thinking he might have been a submissive and you weren't interested in being a switch?"

"Nothing to do with him. This is all about my own fucked-up-ness."

"You're not fucked up," Daniel countered, voice hard with conviction.

"Oh just wait. I didn't tell him...because I didn't trust him."

Daniel felt his protective instincts rear up. "Did he hurt you?"

"I never gave him the chance." Autumn swallowed so hard that even in the shadows he could see her throat working.

"If he knew I was a sexual submissive, he wouldn't respect

me anymore."

Daniel started to call her ex a rude name, but stopped, confused. How did she know how he'd react if she never told him?

"He would think I was stupid and incapable of handling my own life. He would think less of me, and treat me differently."

"Anyone who would do that, think that—"

She held up a hand, cutting him off. "Every man I've ever been with…could ever be with…is the same. I can never tell them I'm a sexual submissive because as soon as they know they'll think less of me. Treat me with disdain."

"Where the fuck are you finding these assholes?" Daniel demanded.

Autumn laughed, but it was a sad sound, a little watery, as if she was holding back tears.

Daniel shifted and ducked his head so he could see her face. Something still wasn't adding up, because she wasn't just talking about her past. She'd said everyone she *could* ever be with.

Tears shimmered on her lower lashes, but her face was dry. The muscles at the corners of her mouth trembled, as if she was fighting the urge to let her lips twist into a sob.

"It's me," she whispered.

"No." He shook his head, kept his gaze on her face. "It's not you—"

"It is, because you see *I'm* the asshole." She raised luminous eyes to his. "I can't bear for men I like, men I might want to date or, worse, might fall in love with, to know I'm a sexual submissive."

She pressed her lips together, then forced herself to smile. "Because deep down I think all submissives, including myself, are weak."

She forced her smile to widen. It was a broken expression. "I hate being a submissive."

CHAPTER 7

Denial. Anger. Confusion. Those were the emotions she was expecting to see on Daniel's face.

Instead he pursed his lips, seeming to consider what she'd just said. She held her breath, but after a moment, he sat back, settling in beside her, so close their upper arms almost touched.

She'd just confessed something hateful, and he had every right to walk away from her. He'd stayed.

"You know you're not an asshole, right?" Daniel said after a moment.

"Oh no, I am. I am a massive asshole."

"Do you respect other subs, even if you think they're weak?"

"It's splitting hairs," she said.

"No. It's not. Do you respect their right to be sexual submissives?"

"Of course. Everyone has a right to their own shit, as long as they're not hurting anyone." She paused. "Or hurting them in a consensual way."

"While you respect their choices, you think their choices are wrong."

"Not wrong but…" She'd come this far, she might as well confess all the rest of her sins. "But every time I see Pet I want to shake her. Tell her to get up. To stop being that way."

Pet was Master Carter's bonded submissive. And he treated her like a pet—she crawled instead of walked. Wore a leash. And outside of Las Palmas their relationship was the same—a 24/7 Master-slave relationship.

"But you don't," Daniel said mildly.

"Of course not."

"You respect her choice," he repeated.

"Okay, yes. I see where you're going with this. I think she is making a stupid choice, but it's her right to make that choice."

"And it's a stupid choice because…?"

"Because I bet that Master Carter doesn't think of her the same way he thinks of say…Gabriela." Gabriela was Master Leo's bonded submissive, and the unofficial head submissive in the club.

"So you think Master Carter probably respects Gabriela, but doesn't respect Pet, his own submissive. And both of them are weak."

"I told you I was an asshole."

"I hate to state the obvious…but I don't think we're talking about Pet right now."

Autumn leaned her head back against the wall. "Yeah, okay. It might not be fully logical. It's just…I hate that I want to submit. That I need to."

"But you do need it?"

"Yes. Trust me, I wish I didn't. I…tried other things." She swallowed hard, trying not to remember. "Didn't work. Las Palmas works for me."

He hummed in quiet acknowledgement, but didn't say anything, so she kept going.

"I had to separate the two parts of my life. Completely separate them. Submission," she said, holding up one hand, "and relationships." She held up the other hand.

"You said you need to submit. How do you handle that with relationships?" He pointed to the hand she'd raised.

"When I am seeing someone, the vanilla sex is always good. I mean I like it, I just need…more."

"Having needs is not weak," he said softly.

She ignored that. "The vanilla sex is probably because I can come here on the weekends and scene. Part of the separation is separating relationship sex from submission sex. And most of the time my scenes don't involve penetrative sex with my top."

"Makes sense," he agreed mildly. "BDSM doesn't have to include sex acts at all."

She nodded, then adjusted his jacket, pulling it closed. Daniel seemed like an intelligent man. He'd probably put the pieces together, but she needed to be explicit. He deserved that, since she'd run away from their scene, which was at best bad BDSM etiquette, and at worst irresponsible because she'd broken a cardinal rule by failing to communicate with her top.

Autumn cleared her throat and steeled herself. "I only scene with people I can keep firmly on this side." She waved her BDSM hand.

He raised his eyebrows in a silent request for her to explain.

"I don't want to bottom for someone I… Someone that makes me feel… Ugh. Are you going to make me say it out loud?" She fought the urge to cover her face. Humiliation and embarrassment bit at her.

"Oh yeah. I want to hear you say it."

His teasing tone lightened the painful embarrassment. She relaxed, and in a haughty tone said, "Jerk."

His only reply was a wide grin, flashing his teeth in the moonlight.

She opened her mouth, but embarrassment choked her once more. After another brief silence he took pity on her.

"If we'd met at that hypothetical bar, we might have hit it off," he summed up. "Might have gone home together for some vanilla sex."

"Yes," she whispered. "And I would have never told you I was a submissive. Because I'd want you to see me as a partner. An equal."

"Not weak," he murmured.

She nodded. "I couldn't tell you because I'd know that, you couldn't both know I was a sub and respect me. You couldn't know I need to be spanked and tied up and hurt and fucked... and respect me."

If you knew I was a sub, you wouldn't love me.

Daniel was silent for a long time. Then he nodded once and pushed to his feet. She closed her eyes so she wouldn't have to watch him walk away.

He didn't leave. When he nudged her bare foot, she cracked open one eye and looked up.

He was silvery in the moonlight, the white undershirt clinging so his chest looked like it was carved of pale stone. He held out his hand and she placed hers in his, letting him help her to her feet.

Without a word he led her back to the warmth and light of the Sub Rosa court, her hand in his. She followed him, blinking in the bright-seeming light from the gas torches and landscape lighting that illuminated the space.

The chair they'd been using was still empty, her discarded corset marking the spot. On the way, Daniel stopped and flipped the lid up on a large basket, pulling out two heavy woven blankets. When they reached the chair, he tossed one of the folded blankets onto the ground.

Autumn swallowed hard. The blankets were often used as cushions so subs could comfortably kneel at their Master or Dom's feet.

She stared at the blanket, anxiety and something like regret churning in her stomach.

Daniel plopped down to sit on the blanket. Autumn blinked at him.

"How about you sit down?" Daniel gestured to the wide chair. "And then tell me who the fucker was who hurt you."

CHAPTER 8

Daniel watched her hesitate, and hoped the rage he felt wasn't showing on his face. He was pretty good about hiding his emotions when needed, but what Autumn had said back there behind the building had pushed him near his damned limit.

Someone had hurt this woman. Someone had made her hate her own submissive needs. He knew, had known, women and girls who were taught not to value themselves. Who'd truly believed themselves to be less. Less worthy, less intelligent. Just...less.

A person's submission was a gift to be treasured. Any Dom, hell, any man in general, who didn't understand that needed to be smacked.

For a minute he thought she'd walk away, and he wouldn't have blamed her. She probably felt emotionally raw.

But eventually she took a seat. Perched on the edge, her knees pressed together, heels of her hands braced on either side of her hips, she was clearly ready to bolt. He handed her the blanket, which she awkwardly draped over her bare knees.

Daniel made a show of stretching out one leg, hoping to

make it apparent that he had every intention of sitting right where he was—it was the least dominant position he could think of. Literally sitting at her feet.

"How about we start with this question," Daniel said. "Did you kill the fucker?"

That startled a laugh out of her, and Autumn relaxed a little, leaning back so she wasn't perched as if prepared for flight.

"No, though my friend offered to kneecap him. It wasn't...he wasn't abusive. Not in the way you're imagining."

"And what do you think I'm imagining?" he asked.

"That I asked a boyfriend to top me and he beat me instead." She fiddled with the hem of the jacket. "It's not quite that linear."

"Help me understand."

Autumn glanced at him from behind her lashes and Daniel's gut tightened.

"I'm still the asshole," she warned. "And I'm a hypocrite."

"No, I don't think you are. Do you think the other subs are stupid?"

She raised a brow. "Of course not."

"And Pet. Do you hate her? Think she's a worthless person."

"No, but I want to shake her. Beg her to stop letting herself be treated like a pet. To stand up and not be..."

"Weak?" he asked, using her word.

She nodded.

"You want her to change her relationship with Master Carter. Want her to quit the 24/7 lifestyle."

"Exactly."

"Why?"

"Because it's...because he'll..." She stammered to a stop.

"Autumn, would you look at me?" He'd been very careful to make that a request and not an order. When she did met his gaze, he held it for a moment before asking the next question.

"Are you angry at Pet because of how she submits...or are you scared for her?"

Autumn sucked in air. Her throat worked and then she bit her lip.

Crap, she was about to cry. Daniel shifted, prepared to get up on his knees and hug her, but stopped himself. Every muscle in his body was tense with the need to comfort her. To protect her.

He always felt at least a little protective of his sub partner. This feeling was something different—a magnitude more than what he'd felt for any other sub.

She was attracted to him. He was attracted to her. Now it was out in the open—a blatant acknowledgement of a romantic attraction, in a place where romance took a back seat to kink.

If they had met in that hypothetical bar he would have left with at the very least her number. At best, with her.

Taken her back to his place for hot passionate sex, and then in the morning, instead of awkward weirdness, they would have ordered in brunch and talked, getting to know one another better before once more falling into bed.

At some point he'd tell her his life story, and then later, when he told her about his sexual needs she'd put two and two together, figure out it equaled 'fucked up', and be gone from his life.

Daniel forced himself to settle back on the blanket, then unclenched his jaw, not wanting to telegraph anger that she might think was directed at her.

"You're right. I'm...scared for her. I'm terrified for all of us." She put one hand over her face, the other wrapped across her middle. "I hadn't realized, until you asked, but you're right. It's fear." Raising her head, she wiped away a tear with the sleeve of his coat, and let out a watery laugh. "I guess that's what I get for not letting myself think about it."

"You're not an asshole," he murmured, aching with the need to hold her.

Another tear fell, and she wiped it away again, then frowned at his sleeve. "I'll have this cleaned for you."

"I don't care about the jacket."

"It's a nice jacket, and now it has concealer on it."

"I really don't give a shit about the jacket. If you want to rub makeup all over it, be my guest."

"Please stop being so…" She waved a hand in the air. "Perfect."

"Perfect?"

She eyed him, the sadness gone, replaced by some of the sass from earlier. "Don't fish for compliments. I already admitted that I find you attractive enough that I was thinking about you as a date rather than a Dom. And then I fully freaked out because of it." She pursed her lips. "And then I confessed my deep dark secret, and you helped me figure out it was a totally different kind of mental health issue than I thought."

Daniel chuckled. "You were right, you know."

"About what?"

Right now Autumn needed a Dom, but not to stimulate her physically. She needed a Dom to protect and cherish her. To make her feel accepted and heard. It was one of the reasons people joined Las Palmas—to be among like-minded individuals, and to have a place where their desires were normal, rather than taboo.

"You were right about what would have happened if we met at that bar."

Autumn's shoulders tightened and she looked away.

"We have chemistry. We have a similar sense of humor—I'm basing that on our conversations so far. So if we had met outside of here, things might have been different." He let his voice deepen. "But this is where we are." He gestured at the courtyard around them.

"Except now you know how messed up my head is." Autumn tried to make it a joke but there was real pain in her words.

If she thought she was fucked up…

Daniel got to his knees. She leaned forward, as if drawn to him, then pulled back.

"What I know is that you're hurting," he said. "That your fear is making you cruel, not to others, but to yourself. You're lying to yourself—"

"I'm not lying to myself."

"Yes." He used his Dom voice this time, deeply pleased when she jumped. "You're telling yourself you're 'an asshole' because of how you feel about submission, but you're not. You're hurting, and that's a defense mechanism."

He braced his hands on either side of her. "You're scared, and you don't trust Dominants."

"Um, clearly I do. I got naked for you within hours of meeting you." Her protest was weak, and she wouldn't meet his eyes.

"You're lying to me, but I'll allow it because you're not doing it intentionally. The primary person you're lying to is yourself."

Her eyes narrowed. "You don't really know me. You can't say—"

He leaned in. Didn't touch her, or say anything, just invaded her personal space. She stopped speaking with a click as her teeth snapped together.

"You might be willing to trust a Dom with your body, but you don't really trust me, or any other top. Not enough to be honest."

"Trusting someone with my body is a damned big deal." She'd raised her chin, looking down her nose at him.

Daniel shifted closer, so his abdomen nearly brushed her knees. "But it's not nearly as important as trusting someone with your emotional truth."

"My emotional truth?" She eyed him. "Are you a psychologist?"

"No, just a man who has been in therapy for years."

"Well here's my emotional truth. I don't like that I need this, but I do need it. I enjoy it too, of course, as long as D/s stuff stays separate from romance."

"That's part of it, but not all of it. It's deeper than that, which is why you displaced some of your feelings onto others, onto submission and being submissive as a whole."

"It's not that complex."

He studied her. "Isn't it? Emotional truth is complicated, because people are complicated. Maybe the term 'emotional truth' is a little dramatic, or too technical, but it's also accurate."

"Maybe, but this isn't therapy." She gestured around.

"Aww come on, Autumn. You're smarter than that." He raised a brow and smiled a little to soften the words. "This place absolutely serves as a therapist's office for some members. Maybe even most of them."

She snorted out a laugh and resettled her hands. Instead of keeping her arms tucked in at her sides, she placed her hands far enough apart that her pinkies brushed against his fingers.

"I want you to submit to me." His words were low, and rougher than he'd intended.

Autumn stiffened, meet his gaze.

"I want you to submit to me knowing that we're attracted to one another. That if we'd met in the vanilla world we might have ended up dating."

Her jaw clenched and she looked away.

"No, Autumn. Look at me." He cupped her chin, forcing her to face him. "You're going to submit, and I'm going to show you that knowing you're a submissive doesn't mean I don't respect you. It doesn't make me any less attracted to you. And if we were to meet in a bar, after this, knowing what I know, I might ask you out on a date."

She jerked back, as if he'd slapped her. That reaction made

him want to reach back through time and find the man or men who'd done this to her and strangle them.

"Why would you say that?" she whispered. "I can't do it…"

"You can. We could test the theory."

That snapped her out of the rising panic he could see on her face. "Theory?"

"Your theory is that now that I know you're a submissive, I won't respect you, correct?"

Autumn arched a brow. "Ah, but now that you know that I think that, you'll pretend to respect me."

"Are you saying you wouldn't be able to tell fake respect from real?" Daniel didn't bother to hide his smile. The banter was fun.

"Hmm, a valid point. I don't think you'll be that good a liar." Her sassy smile faded. "I can feel it when someone…thinks less of me."

Damn it. He didn't want her sad and scared. He wanted her sassy and naked.

"Then we'll proceed with our test. We play the game. You submit. And at the end, when you realize that I don't respect you any less, that I don't think you're any less capable or attractive…you tell me the story."

"What story?"

"The story of who hurt you." He cupped her cheek and when she leaned into his touch his heart clenched, the need to protect her nearly overwhelming.

"Daniel…I'm sorry I ran. I'm sorry I'm an emotional mess, but you don't have to try and fix me."

"I'm not going to fix you, because you're not broken. And even if you were, you're the only one who could make those repairs." He nudged her chin up, waiting until she was looking at him before he smiled. "All I'm going to do is…"

She held her breath, her eyes wide with anticipation. He

could say something moving and dramatic. Something amazing and heartfelt.

But there had been enough emotional drama for the moment. She needed a break from talking, and it was his job, his privilege, to make sure she got what she needed.

"...play with your nipples."

Autumn's eyes widened, and she let out a peal of laughter that had several people looking their way and smiling.

Daniel sat back on his heels, keeping his hands on the bench. He waited for Autumn's laughter to fade to a smile.

"Okay. I want...I want to scene. I want to do the checklist game with you. I can't promise that I won't...that I won't panic."

Daniel gripped her legs, hooking two fingers behind her knees. "If you do, you tell me. One thing I will absolutely demand of you is communication. No more running away rather than talking."

"All right. I can—"

Daniel tightened his grip and yanked her off the chair. She tumbled into his lap, her legs astride his thighs, her arms coming around his shoulders. Her head was still higher than his, but their faces were close enough that all he'd have to do to kiss her was tug her down a few inches.

But a kiss was romantic and intimate. For Autumn, a kiss might once more bring up feelings that, at least for now, were better pushed to the side.

All of which meant he couldn't kiss her.

At least not right now. But in that moment Daniel promised himself that he would kiss this woman. And not as part of a scene.

He was going to kiss her like it was the climactic moment in a romantic movie.

He was going to kiss her like it was their wedding day.

He was going to kiss her because he knew that he could fall

in love with this woman. It was insane, given that he'd known her for only a handful of hours, but that didn't matter.

And maybe it wasn't a question of 'could' he fall for her, but when.

"Autumn," Daniel murmured, forcing his thoughts away from possibilities of if and when. "I want my jacket back."

Her wide eyes met his, and then, much to his dominant delight, she lowered her gaze. He felt her relax, her bodyweight settling on his thighs.

She took one big breath, her chest and shoulders rising. On the exhale she shrugged out of the jacket, letting it fall away.

Leaving her gloriously, submissively naked on his lap

Have you lost your mind? Run. Tonight has already been dramatic and emotional and adding in a full D/s scene will only exacerbate that.

Don't you dare move. You are not going to leave without subbing for this delicious, perfect man.

What are you doing? This is such a bad idea.

Ask him to whip your tits and pussy.

Autumn's internal monologue was having an identity crisis.

It was easy to imagine cartoon devil and angel versions of herself perched on each shoulder. The problem was she wasn't sure whether it was the devil or angel who thought staying to sub for Daniel was a bad idea. On one hand, scening with him might go a long way to helping her deal with her feelings about her own submission, which was a positive thing, so that might mean the angel was pro-subbing to Daniel.

On the other hand staying was a form of emotional, and probably physical, masochism. In that case it was the devil encouraging her to stay.

Daniel had moved them to the chair, and now he leaned

back, laying his arms along the back. It put space between them, and meant her breasts were at his eye level.

Her nipples were hard and tight thanks to the new exposure to the cool air.

"You have lovely breasts and nipples. The piercings are a nice accent." Daniel's voice had deepened with either arousal or dominance. His shoulder muscles were tense, his fingers curling into his palms.

Her own tension ratcheted up to meet his and she watched those muscles, sure that any moment he would make a move. Touch her, grab her.

His breath hissed between his teeth and she watched as he forced himself to relax. Damn it, that was hot. That self-restraint a sign of exactly how in control he was.

"You're scared," Daniel said softly.

That had Autumn sitting up a little straighter. "I'm not scared."

"You are. We just talked about it." His brows rose as a smile touched his lips.

"No, I'm scared *for* the other subs."

"And for yourself."

Right now, she was terrified. Terrified that in breaking her own rules, in scening with him, she would not just reopen old scars, but deepen the wounds.

She could have said that, but she didn't want to talk about her feelings anymore. She needed time to process on her own.

The devil on her shoulder took control. She raised her chin, looking down her nose at him and smirked. "I've played with far more dangerous tops than you."

The smile faded but his brows stayed up. "And how do you know I'm not dangerous?"

She wiggled on his lap. "Hopefully you're the right amount of dangerous."

"Hopefully I'm dangerous enough that, by the time our

weekend is over you will feel well-used and at peace with your submission."

She dropped her gaze to his chest, swallowing hard.

He ducked his head a little to catch her gaze. "And then you'll also see that I still respect you."

Not wanting to meet his eyes, she turned her head.

"You're going to give me everything you have. Submit every part of your body and soul to me."

Autumn's breath hitched, and she was hyper aware of her breasts bobbing in time with her rapid breaths.

"And when it's over, you'll see that I still think you're brilliant and capable. I won't think any less of you, Autumn. Being sexually submissive is courageous. The fact that someone made you think otherwise is a travesty."

"It's not your job to fix my fucked up headspace," Autumn said softly.

"I'm not going to fix you, because you're not broken."

"I am, a little." She smiled wryly.

"No," he snapped in reprimand. "You're wounded. Wounds heal, and there are ways to make them heal faster."

Damn it, he was going to make her cry. And maybe…maybe he was right. If she really submitted to him, and he still respected her, then maybe…maybe it would mean she was okay.

"Any top worthy of the title would do what I'm about to."

A spike of arousal burned through the feelings she was having "And what are you about to do?"

"I'm going to use you." Daniel wrapped his arms around her, jerking her forward so she fell against his chest, her palms on his shoulders, her breasts a hair's distance from his face.

"I'm going to make you submit to me every way I can think of." He turned his head, lips brushing the inner curve of her right breast.

She swayed, trying to angle her nipple across his lips. She was desperate for sensation.

Daniel's hands gripped her waist and he forced her back a few inches. "No."

The reprimand hit her like the lash of a whip and her insides went soft and compliant.

"Your nipples will be played with...sometimes pleasurably, sometimes painfully...when I choose."

"Yes, Sir," she whispered.

"I'm going to use you hard. Because if I don't, if I go easy on you, it won't have as much of an impact."

"Ha."

"Pun intended," he finished.

They were quiet for a moment. Still. It wasn't awkward, but anticipatory.

"If I go easy on you, you won't find it as meaningful if, at the end of the weekend, I ask you out on a nice, normal vanilla date."

"That's your plan to show me you still respect me? A pity date."

"Pity date? Absolutely not what I intend."

"I don't need—"

He didn't let her finish that thought. "You do. We all need something. That's why we spend an obscene amount of money to be members."

"It is a little horrific if you think about it," she murmured.

"Tell me I'm wrong, Autumn. Tell me that you don't need someone to tie you down. Take control. All so that you can let go...and submit."

Her breath caught, her stomach muscles tensed, even as her pussy pulsed with arousal and need.

When she didn't reply he dropped one hand to her leg and squeezed her thigh, hard enough for it to be a reprimand.

"Answer me."

"Yes, Sir." As the last syllable left her lips so did the final remnants of her resistance. Being here with him, like this—in the club, naked on his lap except for the thong—would have pushed her deep into her own subspace long ago, if her attraction to him and the way he made her feel hadn't set off internal alarms.

She'd told him her secret shame, and he hadn't called her a hypocrite. Hadn't walked away from her the way she had from him.

"Ah, there you are," Daniel murmured, the hand on her thigh rising to her cheek. She rested her head in his palm, and he stroked his thumb along her cheekbone.

"On your knees at my feet, please."

CHAPTER 9

Autumn obeyed without letting herself stop and think. Despite the 'please', that had been an order, and the pleasantry somehow underscored his dominance. This was a man who was so in control that he tacked good manners on to his orders and they didn't diminish the unequivocal command in his words.

She knelt on the blanket that she'd had on her lap, close enough to him that her knees were between his toes. Daniel sat forward, brushing her hair back from her face before carefully gathering it into a tail.

She was ready when he abruptly tightened his hold, her scalp lighting up with little prickles of pain. She kept her gaze down as he jerked her head back, only looking up when he ordered her to.

"Something specific happened before. Something changed for you. What was it? Be specific."

His blue-gray eyes bore into hers.

"It was calling me a…a slut." She pressed her nails into her palms. "Not just the word, but your tone of voice, Sir."

"And what was my tone?"

"You sounded...disdainful. Almost degrading. You called me a slut like it was an insult, and it was like...like the man who I had dinner with, who I'd had a good conversation with, disappeared the instant I was on my knees to be spanked." The words came out in a hot rush.

He tucked her hair behind her ear again, his fingers gentle and caring.

"I felt so...embarrassed and stupid. Small and like...like you were going to hit me, hurt me, not just because it was BDSM, but because you saw me as the kind of woman it was okay to hit."

His fingers stilled in her hair. "Never, Autumn. I would never hit you, anyone, in anger or to punish. That is...that is abhorrent to me."

There was something in his voice that told her there was a story there.

After a moment he relaxed with a nearly visible effort. "Someone really did a number on you." He cupped her cheek and she closed her eyes, leaning into his hand once more.

"I told you I was broken," she whispered.

"And I told you that you were not broken." There was steel in his words and voice. "You will not contradict me again."

She bit the tip of her tongue and nodded quickly. "I'm sorry, Sir."

"Oh you will be." Heat suffused his voice.

"Have I earned a punishment?"

"Several."

"Oh." She didn't know if she was worried or turned on. Wait, she was a submissive. She could multitask and be both. Worrying about a punishment was a turn on in and of itself.

"First you're going to be punished for running away from your last punishment. Then you will be punished for using degrading language and being cruel to my submissive."

"Your submissive?" She looked up as he rose. Daniel was

towering over her, his crotch inches from her face as he stood astride her knees.

"You, Autumn. You are my submissive and you were cruel to yourself, weren't you?"

"And the other submissives." Why had she said that?

"Ah, but you weren't. You displaced your fear and anger for, and with, yourself." His gaze was intense. "No more of that. Open your mouth."

Autumn dropped her jaw open, stomach tight with anticipation. Her hands were coming up, ready to unfasten his slacks so he could slide his hard cock into her mouth.

They'd never gotten around to finishing their conversation about intimate touch. Before she'd stalked off, he'd been carefully asking if she was okay with his bare hands on her ass. That was quite a jump from butt-touching to face-fucking, but she wanted it. On her knees with a cock in her mouth was in her sub comfort zone, though she rarely engaged in overtly sexual activities during her scenes.

Daniel's hand tightened in her hair and he jerked her face forward, rubbing his hard cock against her open mouth, the fabric of his slacks and zipper abrading her lips.

When he jerked her back by the hair there was a barely visible damp spot on the front of his pants, and her lips felt a little swollen.

Daniel swung one leg over her head, disappearing briefly while she knelt staring at the seat. He was back before she had time to psych herself into, or out of, anything.

"Up on the chair. Knees on the seat and lean over the back. I want your ass higher than your head."

He was behind her, so she didn't get a chance to see what he was up to. She positioned herself the same way she had before—her midsection leaning on the back of the chair, fingers under her, elbows sticking up, arms tucked against her sides.

Cool, smooth rope—she knew what it was just by the weight and feel of it—draped over her back.

"Unfortunately, you cannot be trusted to stay still for your punishment." He wrapped the rope, loosely, around her midsection and then, after removing the pillow back and tossing it aside, laced the ends through the slatted wooden back of the chair, bringing it up and around her forearms and wrists in a wide, loose cuff, before threading it back through to the front.

"I won't run this time, Sir."

"No, you won't." He tied off the restraint. "Because I'm not giving you a choice."

He teased her ass with the ends of the rope, making them dance across her skin before releasing them. He came around and crouched so they were eye to eye. Her hair was falling around her face, but he carefully tucked it behind her ears.

"Remember, I don't use a slowdown code word. I will, of course, respect your safe word—pickle—but if you need to slow down, or are uncomfortable, say so."

"You want open and honest communication." She repeated his earlier words.

He smiled up at her, and she was so entranced with his smile that she didn't notice his hand move.

But she felt it when he cupped her dangling breast, massaging it gently. Autumn's eyes fluttered closed on a moan.

"Autumn, I am going to touch you in overtly sexual ways, as part of our scene. I think it's necessary. Do you understand?"

"Yes, Sir."

"And yes, I'm aware we should have had this discussion before I put you into a submissive position, but you needed to be pulled out of your own head more than you need to negotiate the scene to death."

"Thank you." She opened her eyes. "I mean that, Daniel. Thank you, because I did want…need…to get out of my own head."

"I will wear gloves for any penetration done with my fingers, and for tonight my cock is staying in my pants."

She opened her mouth to protest. She wanted him to face fuck her. She had been ready, and more than willing, when he put her on her knees a few moments ago.

"No." He pinched her nipple, hard enough to make her yelp. "That would cross a line, and besides…" He leaned in. "It's not your decision to make, is it?"

"No, Sir."

"Good."

He switched breasts, quickly kneading that one, before pinching the nipple.

Next he carefully removed her piercings. The gentle, precise brush of his fingers as he unscrewed the ball and slid the bar free made her pant. When both were removed, he tucked them into his pocket.

He bent to examine her now fully naked breasts. Not that she hadn't been naked before, but there was a different kind of intimacy in having her jewelry gone. In knowing that he'd done so because he was going to do things to her breasts and nipples that couldn't happen with the piercings in place.

He stroked her. "You have lovely breasts."

Her breath caught again, her eyes meeting his. For a moment Daniel swayed forward, and she thought he'd kiss her, but he stopped short. His sigh was heavy, and when he turned his head away she could see the muscle in his jaw working as he once more fought to control himself.

"I'll be back in a moment."

He pushed to his feet and was gone before the last word was fully spoken.

Autumn hung her head to let her neck muscles rest, and though she told herself not to think about it, her mind turned to thoughts of kissing Daniel. It wasn't that she'd never kissed or been kissed by BDSM partners before, but the kisses were different. A kiss on the forehead or cheek, often done in tandem with a comforting hug in aftercare.

Pop culture BDSM was all about the sexual aspect of the play, but that was rare in public clubs or munches, and even here, where privacy and loose rules meant more overtly sexual play, many people were happy without it. It was how she preferred it.

Until Daniel.

She was changing everything for him. She could lie to herself and say it was part of the game, but it was Daniel. If it had been anyone but him who used that tone on her she would have been irritated, but not so distressed that she had to walk away.

Before her thoughts could spiral, he was back. Daniel's hand slid over the curve of her ass and down her thigh. Next he shifted the rope tails off her ass.

Clearing the way for the spanking that she knew was coming.

Autumn lifted her head and twisted her neck enough to look back at him. She could only hold it for a moment, but it was enough to see that he was holding a black and neon green flogger.

Her toes curled in nervous anticipation and she shifted her weight from knee to knee, the rope pulled tight by her movement, the pressure of the bondage delicious.

"Count for me," he commanded.

Thwap. The first strike hit her ass and it was a nice thud of a good, soft-tailed flogger.

"One," she breathed.

"How many do you think you've earned?"

"I'm not trying to be a brat when I say this, but I really don't think I should answer that."

"And why not?"

"Because if I guess too low, you'll punish—"

Thwap.

"Ahh, two."

"You were saying?" Daniel asked politely.

"If it's too low you'll punish me, and if I guess high, you'll—"

Thwap.

"Three, Sir."

"Well done. Though I'd like you to finish your sentence."

Thwap, thwap.

"Four, five." The heat was building now, and that last one had been hard enough to really register as pain.

"It's rather distracting to have you keep stopping in the middle of sentences."

Thwap.

"Six. Ouch."

"Ouch, what?"

"Ouch, Sir."

"Well done. Now, please finish what you were trying to say."

"If I guess a high number, you'll decide to do that many, instead of whatever you were going to do." She spoke as fast as she could, the words running together.

Thwap.

"Seven. Sir."

"Did that one not hurt enough?" He sounded politely curious.

She looked over her shoulder, shot him a wide-eyed look.

He smirked at her, and it was weird and wonderful to have him flip from serious and precise to teasing.

"Never fear," he assured her. "I can fix that."

The next two strikes were hard, the tails of the flogger spreading out to cover both ass cheeks, striking already reddened and sensitized skin.

She yelped, her heels kicking up until she almost touched her ass.

"Relax." Daniel's voice was back to all business.

He rested the flogger on her back, and then his strong fingers dug into the muscles of her shoulders, forcing them down away from her ears. "Don't tense up. Stay soft. Accept your punishment."

He put one knee on the bench beside her, his pants brushing her leg, his warm body touching the curve of her ass as he leaned down over her to whisper in her ear.

"If you're tense, you're fighting the punishment. You're not going to do that, because you know you deserve this. Need this."

He reached under her, finding one of her hanging, vulnerable breasts. His thumb flicked her nipple, and when she started to tense in reaction to the instant pleasure, his other hand slapped her ass.

His hand was harder, the strike less dispersed than the flogger. That one hurt.

She cried out in pain. A pain that was coupled with pleasure when he gently grasped her nipple and rolled it between two fingers.

Her pussy clenched, and she knew the fabric of her thong was soaked. She'd opted for laser treatment to remove her pubic hair, and could feel the wet fabric clinging to her vulva.

"How many lashes from the flogger do you need, Autumn?"

He switched to the other breast, rolling that nipple with exquisite precision.

She barely registered his question. The pleasure from her nipples mingled with the pain of the flogging. Instinctually, she spread her knees, offering her pussy.

He picked up the flogger and she tensed in anticipation. She wasn't sure if she was terrified or thrilled at the idea of the flogger tails striking her pussy, but whichever emotion it was, the thought also made her throb with arousal.

She didn't realize she tensed again, arching her back and

pushing up against the ropes, until he used the hand that had been gently tugging her nipples to force her head down.

"Relax your shoulders. Drop your head."

There was no choice but to obey as his hand, tangled in her hair, pushed her down.

The back of the chair dug into her ribs. Her back muscles were starting to hurt, and her ass throbbed, though the heat from the flogging was already fading.

He slid off the chair, releasing her hair. The loss of his body heat made her shiver.

The tips of his now slightly dusty black shoes appeared in the limited field of vision she had thanks to her hair falling around her face. He gathered her hair, more gently than a moment ago, and used it to tug her head up, so that while her shoulders were lower than her ass, she was looking out, towards the horizon line. Though in this case there was no horizon to see, only some pretty plants and through the breaks in the leaves, a couple seated together on the twin to the chair she currently knelt upon.

Daniel plucked the flogger off her back. He swung it several times, snapping it against his lower leg. Then he did several underhand practice swings, bringing the flogger up from below rather than across in a horizontal motion.

"I'm going to flog your breasts, Autumn."

Her eyes widened and she twisted as much as she could, given her position and his hold on her hair.

"Take a deep breath. Good. Again. Now keep your chin up."

"Sir, I'm not sure how much longer I can hold this position." She wasn't sure she'd be able to hold it at all once he started flogging her breasts.

"This is a stress posture," he agreed. "I won't ask you to hold it for long."

"Thank you, Sir."

Daniel released her hair, which fell over one shoulder alongside her neck, the twisted strands more controlled thanks to his handling.

"Don't count. All I want you to do is feel."

She couldn't see his face, only his body from midsection down. Her vision narrowed in on his hand and the flogger, which he was casually swinging at his side.

She knew the first strike was coming, saw him pull his hand back a little further than he had before. She took a breath, held it, and in the second before the flogger made contact, she closed her eyes.

The soft tails smacked against her hanging breasts, and one crossed directly over her tight left nipple.

The strike didn't hurt, nor did it feel good. It was simply pure sensation. A firm caress that covered both breasts.

"Breathe," Daniel commanded.

The flogger struck her breasts again, and again. He shifted position, so that each part of her breasts was able to experience a strike from a different position. There was pleasure where the massed center of the tails struck. A slight pinch where the tip landed.

She'd had her breasts flogged before, even cropped once, but both those times she'd been standing. This was different, because she was so deliciously vulnerable. Her nipples defenseless, the soft underside of her breasts getting as much attention as the tops.

Her breasts felt full and heavy, her nipples hard not just with the cold, but from need. Her areolae were no longer contracted, but warm enough from the flogging to have relaxed.

Dimly, she was aware that she was whimpering, the sound soft and animalistic.

"You're doing beautifully," Daniel praised, moving again.

The flogger found virgin skin and she dropped her head as she moaned in response to the sweet caress. Her skin was now sensitive enough that even these soft blows from a gentle flogger were starting to hurt.

"No, no, head up."

She heard him, but it was dim and distant. Her world had shrunk to the feeling of the flogger on her breasts, of cool air hitting the wet fabric of her panties. Of her ass high in the air, her breasts dangling and vulnerable.

"Head. Up."

He punctuated the words with rapid, hard blows from the flogger. Now it was undeniably pain, and the tip of one lash had landed directly on her right nipple. Her pussy pulsed in reaction, even as she cried out.

She raised her head, neck and back straining.

Once more Daniel sank to a crouch in front of her. Eyes on her face, he reached up to cup and fondle each breast.

"Your tits are nicely pink. And warm. Nipples…" He tweaked one and she sucked in air between her teeth. "…very sensitive."

He pushed up. "You can relax now."

She let her head drop, her whole body slumping, as she took heavy breaths.

His fingers worked the rope, untying the knot and then helping her ease up until she was kneeling on the chair. Daniel cupped her cheek, tipping her face up.

"Now it's time to talk about your nipples…and what name I'm going to call you."

CHAPTER 10

Daniel nudged Autumn off the chair, steadying her as she stood. He kept her there only long enough for him to take a seat, then tugged her down so she was once more kneeling, but now straddling his lap.

He had a very nice view of her slightly pink breasts.

The lighting outdoors wasn't ideal for differentiating colors of flesh, but even if they'd been in a pitch black room he would have been able to feel the effects of the flogging thanks to the warmth in her skin.

Cupping her breasts, he thumbed her nipples, indulging himself for a moment by simply playing with her pretty tits, before raising his gaze to her face.

"Arms up, behind your head," he murmured.

She obeyed instantly.

"One of our items is name change. I'd planned to ignore it, but now I have a better idea."

She looked down at him, soft and open. Her lips were slightly parted and he could see the tip of her pink tongue. Her lower lip was damp—she must have bit or licked it while he was playing with her nipples.

"You're probably not going to like it," he warned her. "But this isn't about what you like, is it?"

"No, Sir."

"It's about what you need."

He was walking a very thin line with what he was about to do. He wouldn't have risked it with anyone else. But Autumn needed this, and he needed to make her feel whole, see herself for the amazing, beautiful woman that she was.

Autumn feared her own needs. In a way he thought she probably hated herself, though she hadn't come out and said it as baldly as that. But that was the heart of her fear.

He knew something about hating oneself, and a whole lot about fear. He needed to help her with this the same way he needed to give her pleasure. He knew that one person couldn't fix another, but he could, and would, help her.

"For the rest of the weekend I will not be using your name." He made his words hard and cold. "I will be referring to you as what you are."

Autumn went still.

"Pet. Slut. Whore." The words were cold, cruel, and she flinched away from him.

He gave her a minute, but she didn't say anything.

"Maybe I'll be kind and let you pick what I call you." He pinched one nipple, twisting until she hunched her shoulders, instinctively trying to break his hold.

"No," he snapped, releasing the nipple only to slap her breast.

She flinched and whimpered, and the dark place inside him that needed this—needed to cause pain—crowed in delight.

He was a monster in an elegant suit. But he was a monster who was also very self-aware, and totally in control.

"I hate those words, Daniel." Her voice was barely above a whisper, and she'd turned her face away.

"Are they hard limits?" He didn't remember seeing them on her checklist.

"No. I just…If I hear a Dom using any of those words, I put him in the 'never scene with him list.'"

"You avoided the issue, rather than formally put them on your hard limit list, or discuss them in scene negotiation."

"Yes."

When he touched her cheek, she looked at him. Tears gathered on her lashes.

This was the critical moment, where he had to show her that nothing would change how he saw her. Would make her any less.

Maybe he needed her to understand that, believe that, because he needed a reassurance that he wasn't really a monster. In his case it would be false comfort.

She looked at him with such vulnerability that he knew the next thing he said would be critical. That if he misspoke he could trigger an emotional landmine.

Daniel winked. It wasn't a sensual wink, but a comedic, overblown thing where he scrunched up half of his face.

Autumn sputtered out a surprised laugh.

"You know what they say, sticks and stones may break your bones." He cupped her waist, squeezing gently. "But words will cause deep psychological trauma and create weird sexual kinks."

Autumn dissolved into laughter, whooping with amusement. He laced his hands together behind her back to brace her and stop her from tumbling off the chair.

And through it all, she kept her hands behind her head, arms raised with her elbows out.

That was telling.

More specifically it was telling him that the laughter hadn't drawn her all the way out of the scene. Hopefully it had been a brief emotional release, enough of one that she would be able to handle what he had planned.

And if she wasn't ready, they'd keep circling around it. He could be patient when needed, and Autumn deserved that.

He waited for her laughter to fade down to a smile before he spoke again.

"You might not like those words, at least in the abstract," he said lightly. "But you'll like them when I use them."

She swallowed, but didn't look away.

"I didn't like it when you called me a slut before," she whispered.

"Was it my words or my tone?"

"Both. Mostly your tone."

"Then I see no reason not to refer to you as my pretty little pet."

He used the cultured, formal voice that had, through a lot of hard work, become his normal speaking voice. She didn't react, so he kept going.

Daniel stroked her side several times. "Or perhaps I'll call you my needy little slut." He slid his hand down her belly, and let his thumb briefly rest on her thong, over her pussy, just touching, no caress or stimulation.

"Or my submissive whore." He could see the way her stomach muscle clenched in response to even small stimulus.

"Damn it," she whispered.

"Talk to me."

"It's...It's hot when you say it, but..."

"But it still makes you nervous. That's fine." With a nudge he directed her off his lap. "Spread your legs."

She stepped wide, now in a standard and undeniably submissive posture—arms up and out of the way, feet wide apart.

"On second thought, I'm going to use all three words, depending on my mood. Sometimes I'll be kind, and you'll be my pet. When you're writhing and desperate for me to fuck you, you'll be my needy little slut."

He added the faintest hint of a sneer to the words, and carefully watched her expression. It didn't change. She didn't flinch or jerk.

"And when you're so submissive that you'll do anything I ask, let me do anything I want to your body…then I'll call you 'whore'."

She shifted her weight from foot to foot, hips rocking.

"Talk to me. What are you thinking, pet?"

"I'm thinking I shouldn't be turned on by this."

"But you are."

She nodded, though he hadn't actually asked a question.

"It should freak me out even *more* to hear you say those words, use them, after we talked." Her gaze, which had been focused on his chest, rose to meet his. "But I'm not. I even…I want it."

"Want to be my pet? My slut?" He drew designs on her inner thighs with the tip of one finger and watched her leg muscles clench in reaction.

"I don't have a degradation kink." Her voice was almost pleading.

"No, I don't think you do. But I think you have let fear limit your play, because you didn't feel safe."

"I trust and respect the men I've scened wi—"

Her words cut off on a gasp as he cupped her pussy. Using his middle finger he pressed the satin between her labia. The wet fabric molded to the inside of her sweet cleft. He stroked that same finger over the bump of her clit and her whole body jerked in response.

He ran his nail over her clit, as if he were scratching it, knowing that the fabric would protect her enough to keep the sensation from veering too far into the pain section of that particular gauge.

"Holy fuckidy shit," she whimpered, thighs twitching.

His lips quirked with amusement and pleasure. Pleasure that

in this moment she was still the woman who'd boldly referred to the checklist game as "bat-shit" crazy. He wanted it all from her. Wanted the sass coupled with submission.

He scratched her clit again, and her whole body jerked. She dropped her hands, grabbing his shoulders to keep herself up.

When he did it a third time she whimpered and started to close her legs.

"No, slut." He punctuated the reprimand with a vicious pinch to her nipple.

She sucked in air between her teeth, then let it out as a low, aroused moan.

"Arms up. Show off your tits."

Eyes half closed, she obeyed. He ran his thumbs over the pale flesh on the underside of each breast.

"I like your arms up, elbows bent, because it lifts your breasts." His own patience was nearing a breaking point, so he leaned in and licked each nipple, wetting the skin. "Right now you're presenting your tits to me."

"Yes, Sir."

"You're my needy slut, aren't you?"

She whimpered, her eyes opening enough that she could look down at him.

"You like showing off your lovely breasts. Like making it easy for me to pinch and hurt them."

She took a deep, bracing breath. "Yes, Sir."

"And why do you like that?"

"Don't make me say it…"

He slapped her tits, spanking them right on the nipple. Four strikes on each breast, alternating. She cried out and hunched her shoulders a little, but her hips rolled forward and back in a needy undulation.

"Why do you like it when I pinch your nipples and slap your breasts?"

There was no right answer, only her answer. What her

answer was would tell him where he needed to take the scene next.

"I like it because I'm your slut."

There was a slight stress on the word 'your'. He gave himself a minute to process that, quickly running through potential next moves, before cupping her tits and massaging them.

"That's right. You're my slut."

It was that possessive phrasing, coupled with a cool, accepting tone, that had turned a word she'd run from before into one that visibly aroused her.

She caught her lower lip between her teeth and bit down so hard that her skin turned pale. She was looking for more stimulus.

He grabbed her by the hips and yanked her forward. She shuffled her feet, managing to maintain her balance. His knees were now between her thighs, her tight nipples inches from his face. His cock was diamond-hard in his pants.

She wasn't the only one affected by the possessive phrase. Every dominant urge in his body roared in triumph. She *was* his. This complex, complicated woman who was scared but courageous, hated her own needs but indulged in them with gusto.

Daniel buried his face between her breasts, taking a deep breath. Her skin smelled like lotion, talcum powder, and her own unique scent.

Turning his head to the side, he nipped her breast, pinching skin between his teeth. That felt good, satisfied a primal need to both give her pain and mark her.

He leaned back, cupped her left breast, and then bit the upper curve. Holding the flesh between his teeth he sucked, drawing blood into the trapped skin. It had been a long time since he'd deliberately given someone a hickey. An irritating little voice inside his head was pointing out how juvenile this was, but he didn't care.

He wanted her marked, but he had no right to leave her with

bruises or welts from impact play. So instead he would leave his mark on her breasts. Declare them his personal property.

"You're mine," he murmured, kissing the splotchy wet spot he'd just left on her tit.

Pinching the apex of one breast—compressing nipple, areola, and more between his fingers and thumb—he lifted her breast and fastened his teeth to the soft underside.

It was harder to get a good bite here, because her skin was taut, but his attempts—which resulted in a few pinching bites before he managed to get a mouthful—wrung cries of pleasure and pain from Autumn.

Satisfied, he sat back while still holding the tit up. She was standing tall, no doubt to alleviate the pull. Her eyes were half closed, lips parted and damp.

Satisfied with his handiwork, he released her breast, giving it a reward pat, before turning his attention to its twin.

This time, he wasn't so gentle.

Autumn yelped when his teeth bit down. Whimpered when he lifted this breast so he could bite and mark the underside. Whimpered because this time he lifted by the nipple only.

When he was done using his teeth he once more leaned back. He began to roll her nipple against the side of his index finger with his thumb. All while still lifting, the weight of her breast adding pressure to her nipple.

"Sir, please," Autumn cried out.

"What do you need, pet?" He watched her carefully when he used the word. He'd chosen it because she'd mentioned Master Carter's 24/7 partner Pet in her confession. The word would have connotations for her, but at the same time, it was also almost an endearment. A—haha—pet name.

"It hurts, Sir."

"And does my slut like it when it hurts?"

She blinked, then looked down, seeking his gaze. "Do you like hurting me?"

Yes, because I'm a monster.

"It's my right, my privilege, to give you what you need." He surprised himself with the intensity of his words. "And you need pain. You need to be pleasured and punished. Not punished for your desires. Punished for the way you treat yourself." He hadn't meant to get that deep.

Autumn was looking down at him with a soft hope that made his heart hurt. Made him burn with a need that wasn't physical.

"You need to be my pet. My slut. My whore." He enunciated the words, making them hard, but not derogatory.

"Just for you," she whispered.

Their gazes met and held for a long moment. She looked away first, and he was both disappointed and relieved.

"Arms down," he commanded.

She shook out her hands as she relaxed her upper body. Her legs stayed spread—not that she had much choice given that she was straddling his knees. She'd wiggled around just enough while he was biting and sucking her tits that the fabric of her thong had worked its way further between her labia. The puffy, slick lips were protruding lewdly on either side of the dark fabric.

He wanted to strip it off her and bury his face between her legs the way he'd done with her breasts. Maybe even bite and suck her pussy, leave her marked down there.

But he couldn't put his mouth on her vulva, or use his bare fingers to fuck her vagina. That was a level of intimacy outside the scope of this scene.

There were plenty of other things he could, and would, do to her.

He reached between her legs and once more ran his nail over her clit. Her hands fisted at her sides as she threw her head back, thrusting her hips forward.

"Very good, slut." He patted her pussy affectionately,

watching to see how she reacted to the word slut without "my" in front of it.

"Thank you, Sir," she murmured in the smooth, even tones of a submissive who was deep in their subspace.

"On your knees, legs spread. Sit back on your heels." He waited for her to drop into the position, her legs splayed on either side of his feet. He carefully raised the toe of one shoe and rubbed it against her pussy.

When he pulled back the leather was damp.

"What a good whore to polish my shoes with your cunt." He tucked her hair behind her ear, pairing crude words with a tender gesture.

She turned her face into his hand, rubbing her parted lips against his palm. There was no cringing withdrawal or teary eyes.

What Autumn needed was to be used while also being cherished—not one thing followed by the other. With another sub, it might have been harder to offer that level of care, because he would have had to fake it to some degree. Not with Autumn.

Enough feelings shit.

He was in complete agreement with his inner voice.

The flogging he'd given her ass and tits had been gentle, meant to warm her up for what was to come, while also setting the tone for the scene. He wanted to pull her over his lap and spank her ass until she was shrieking in protest, her legs kicking in the air, butt red and tender.

They might get to that. The night was still young, even accounting for the time they'd spent talking behind the building. Maybe he would get to spank her tonight. Maybe he could leave her butt sore and aching to go along with the bite marks on her tits.

Fantasizing about that was not helping his control, and his cock was already so hard that he was pretty sure there would be a zipper imprint on it when he finally took his pants off.

Daniel gripped her gently by the throat, waited until her eyes met his. "Stay like this, pet. I have a few things I'm going to get."

She nodded, chin bumping his fingers.

"What a good little whore you are." He rubbed his thumb against her lower lip to soften the words.

"Yes, Sir."

Daniel rose, grimacing as his cock rubbed against his fucking pants. He swung one leg over her head, and made his way to the Den.

He had some very specific toys in mind. If he found what he was looking for, Autumn's ass, pussy, and nipples would all soon be throbbing.

And if she was a very good girl he might even let her come.

CHAPTER 11

P*et.*
   Slut.
Whore.

The words created a tight knot in her stomach. One that hadn't been there when Daniel was present, but he'd left her with her thoughts as company. Her thoughts were not always the kindest companions.

When she spoke the words in the quiet of her mind, they were spat with derision. That wasn't how he'd used them. Coming from Daniel they'd been, if not exactly compliments, almost accolades. Like being called a 'bitch.'

That thought made her smile. She considered it a point of pride the first time a man had called her a bitch for being—in his mind—too aggressive. Too successful.

"Smiling? I like that."

She'd heard footsteps—not the first set to walk along the path behind her—but hadn't realized it was Daniel until he spoke.

She twisted to look at him, maintaining her kneeling, palms up posture.

Daniel was carrying a massive duffle bag. He eased it gingerly off his shoulder. It was clearly heavy, and when he set it down there was an audible thump.

Autumn glanced from him to the bag and back again. "Do you have...a body in there?"

He straightened, putting his hands on his hips. He'd changed out of his suit pants and undershirt, putting on a pair of Dom leathers and boots, along with a black tank top. He was pulling off the man in black look very, very well.

"A dead body? No. Luckily, necrophilia isn't one of our assigned N words."

"Good lord." She knew she was making a face. "Well I'm pretty sure even if it was, I would have marked that one with a big, fat no."

He stepped over the bag and took a seat on the bench and carefully maneuvered one heavy boot between her legs. She sucked in air, wondering if he was going to use her very wet pussy to shine his boot.

She was certainly wet enough, and as degrading as it was, she wanted his foot nudging her pussy. Not because she had a degradation kink, but because she was so aroused, she'd take any stimulation. At least, if he was the one doing it. Anyone else...well, that was a different story.

"Now if we're talking about a live body—"

She had to jerk her attention away from his boot—and fantasies about its possible application to her pussy—to his face, and then to the duffle bag.

"Maybe I had another sub climb in there, and they're the toy I'm going to use on you." He leaned down, a smile tugging the corner of his lips and his eyes sparkling with sexy, dominant amusement. "Would you like that? Having another sub laying under you, their tongue teasing your clit each time I ordered them to lick you. I wouldn't let you come like that, of course."

She shivered, one of those full body shivers that made her shoulders twitch and her areolas puckered in tight.

"Oh, you like that idea."

She arched a brow. "What's not to like, Sir?"

He laughed, grabbed her gently by the neck, and pulled her in so he could lean down and kiss the top of her head.

Oh.

Oh.

When he released her and stood to go open the duffle, Autumn didn't turn around. That little peck on the head had left her…stupefied.

She'd walked away from him before because he was the kind of man she could fall in love with, and because of that she couldn't stand for him to see her being submissive.

When he'd kissed her head like that…a quick, spontaneous, affectionate gesture…she'd realized that he wasn't just the kind of man she *might* develop romantic feelings for.

She was catching feelings. She was falling for him.

Crap.

Her internal panic distracted her enough that she didn't notice when he took the heavy half-barrel-shaped piece of equipment out of the bag. She tuned back in only when the buzz of vibration distracted her.

She glanced over and her eyes went wide.

Daniel had brought out a Sybian. The half cylinder covered in black vinyl was just over a foot high and about that wide. He'd set it up in the center of a woven blanket, which he'd spread out beside where she knelt.

As she watched he disappeared, holding a rather incongruous thick orange extension cord, which he was unlooping as he walked.

He returned a few moments later, apparently having found someplace to plug the Sybian in.

While he was gone Autumn had tried to see what else was in

the bag, in particular what attachments he'd brought for the Sybian—sometimes called a saddle masturbator or just "a saddle". At the apex of the curved machine was a small ridge, with a circular opening where a short metal shaft could be attached, though it wasn't currently screwed in. The various attachments were fitted onto the raised ridge, and, if there was a dildo on the attachment it fit over the metal shaft.

She'd only played with one once. And though it had been here at the club, it hadn't been as part of a scene. One of the overseers had developed a new type of attachment and had asked for volunteer subs to test it out.

The orgasm had been quick and gasp-inducing, thanks to the o-shaped clit stimulator.

However, that time she'd been in charge of the controller, and chosen how long she wanted to spend in that particular saddle.

This was going to be very different, she was sure.

Daniel took a seat, leaning forward so his elbows were on his knees, his head turned to the side to look at her. He was smiling, and it was the same delicious smile she'd seen at dinner. No sneer or smirk. A real smile.

The tight knot of worry low in her gut loosened.

"Have you ridden one of these before?" He leaned down and picked up the controller, a box slightly larger than a game controller, with a long black wire connecting it to the Sybian.

"Once. But I was in charge of that." She pointed at the controller box.

"This is mine." He pressed it possessively to his chest, then smiled. "This is going to be fun."

"I think so too, Sir."

He hooked one booted foot in the strap of the duffle bag, pulling it closer. She waited for him to pull out an attachment or overlay, but he didn't reach into the bag.

His gaze swept down her, and the air around them thickened. Her breath caught, her nipples tingled, and she knew that when he spoke again his words would be a low-toned command.

"Stand up and strip, pet."

Autumn pushed to her feet, bracing her hands on the ground. Normally she could do it without having to use her hands—a pride point among the submissives, and the only reason she tortured herself with squats and deadlifts—but she'd been kneeling long enough that the support was necessary. Daniel didn't reprimand her, the way beginner and fake Doms would have. He reached out, cupping her elbow as she rose. Once she was steady he reached down and massaged her lower legs, helping to restore the circulation.

"Thank you, Sir."

"I have to take care of my slut, don't I?" His hands slid up her legs to her hips.

He toyed with the straps of her thong. Now that she was standing she could feel the bunched, sodden fabric of her thong between her labia, an awkward, uncomfortable feeling that made her hyper aware of her pussy, and slightly embarrassed by how it must look.

Daniel gripped the straps of her thong and yanked up. Autumn shrieked in surprise, then hissed in pain as the fabric was forced tight against her anus and pussy.

"I told you to take this off, didn't I?" He reached around and grabbed the back, pulling so that the fabric sawed against her sensitive flesh.

It hurt in all the right ways, and Autumn danced up onto her toes, her hands hanging awkwardly at her sides.

Daniel released it, and before she'd fully lowered herself back onto her heels he was grabbing the thong and shoving it down. It clung to her pussy and removing it stimulated her clit just enough that she let out a little moan.

Daniel surged to his feet, grabbed her hair, forcing her head back. "Did you enjoy me hurting your cunt like that, whore?"

"No…"

Daniel arched a brow and smiled in amusement. "No?"

Autumn leaned into him, her bare breasts rubbing his chest, even as her scalp started to burn with pain.

"I'd like to change my answer."

"By all means, go ahead."

"Yes, Sir. I enjoyed it."

"Then why did you lie?"

She shrugged, only to yelp when his hand switched from her hair to her neck and he yanked her back, putting space between them. His cheek brushed hers as his lips found her ear.

"Did you lie because you were upset by being called a whore?"

"No, Sir."

"Were you lying to yourself, too?"

"Not exactly."

"Then why?"

"Because I didn't want you to do it again. Not because…not because I was scared of the pain, but because I wanted the scene to move on." The words escaped in a rush, and she tensed, anticipating the fallout.

His thumb slid up to press on the soft spot behind her ear, a strange, intimate touch, before he released her.

Daniel stepped back and sat, casually crossing his legs, ankle on knee. "You are impatient for the pleasure you assume I'll allow you to feel, because of the toy I brought."

"I—"

"Quiet, slut." He waited, brow raised.

She stayed silent, having to clench her teeth to manage it.

"Good to see you can behave."

She felt like a student called to the principal's office—she'd been caught and now she'd be reprimanded.

And damn it she was so fucking wet. Without the thong, her slick pussy lips rubbed against one another any time she shifted her weight. Her nipples ached with the need for stimulation, and she had to clench her hands into fists to stop herself from reaching up to play with herself.

This scene, the time she was spending with Daniel, was headed down paths and into areas she'd never thought she wanted to go. That she'd never planned on enjoying. Schoolgirl role-play normally made her cringe, and yet at this moment she wished she had on a plaid skirt, and he was seated behind a desk.

She'd never trusted a—

Trust. She froze, all her attention turned inward. She trusted Daniel. A man she'd only just met, but after a handful of hours knew her shameful secret, and didn't find her horrible or disgusting. She trusted him in a way she hadn't trusted someone in a very long time.

"Hey."

She blinked, focusing. Daniel was standing once more, peering at her face. His gaze moved over each feature as if he could decode her thoughts. Maybe he could.

"Talk to me," he said softly.

"I...trust you."

The corners of his eyes crinkled in a smile, but his mouth stayed soft. "I don't think you trust people very often, do you?"

"No, I don't. It...surprised me. To realize how much I trust you."

"And I'm honored by that trust. And at some point I would appreciate a full rundown of the thought process that got you there, but that's a conversation for aftercare." He touched her chin, then ran his fingers down the center line of her body all the way to her pussy.

With every millimeter he stroked, she slid deeper into scene. Into her submission.

By the time his knuckle gently prodded the plump top of her vulva, she felt soft and willing. Wildly aroused.

"Thank you, Sir," she murmured.

"For?"

"For using me. For giving me what I need."

"You're very welcome, pet." He stepped back. "Now it's time to get you ready to ride." He winked in that silly exaggerated way that made her smile.

When he turned to the bag there was only one dark thought that she couldn't fully put aside.

He knew so much about her…but she knew nothing about him.

SHE WAS PERFECT.

No, not perfect. Perfect wasn't real. No person could be perfect.

What Autumn was, was perfect *for him*.

He'd never felt so in tune with a submissive before. Somehow he could look at her and he just knew. What she was feeling, what she needed.

And the way that they both were able to slide from a heavy D/s vibe to a lighter, companionable moment and back again was astonishing. In the past, pulling back from that place where he kept his need for control, from his Dom persona, into being just Daniel would disrupt the energy of the scene.

With her it didn't.

With her he felt…whole. Like he could be wholly himself. And that meant he wanted to tell her about his past.

The overseers knew, due to the club vetting process, and while the shittiest parts of his childhood were readily accessible to anyone willing to google, he didn't talk about them. He'd accepted his own past, thanks to years of therapy, and he still went every other week, but while his therapist had helped him process his trauma, he hadn't been totally forthcoming with them about how heavily into D/s he was.

He hadn't told his therapist, because he knew what they would say. He'd point out that Daniel's deep need for control was an understandable coping mechanism, given what had happened to him. In other aspects of his life he'd worked on giving up control. On letting other people take charge, even if that gave him anxiety.

The one place he hadn't tried to adjust his behavior was when it came to BDSM. He didn't want to be told that the healthiest thing for him would be to walk away from the lifestyle, and he was absolutely certain that would be the primary suggestion.

He couldn't give up being a Dom, but he had pushed himself to be more of a service top. The best scenes were ones where the submissive got what she needed.

Outside of the club he was in control, but not controlling. He never let his Dom side come out to play, unless he was safely within the Las Palmas gates.

Earlier he'd thought about asking her out. Romantic thoughts fueled by moonlight, tied in with the desire to help her, even rescue her from her own demons.

What he was feeling right now was far less romantic. It was something deeper and more complicated.

Their innate compatibility meant something. This connection between them was the reason she was letting him deliberately push her boundaries as a submissive.

Why she'd trusted him with her secrets.

And that was the problem. Because he wanted, for the first time in a very long time, to tell someone about his past. He wanted to sit beside her in the dark and let the words flow.

But doing that would break this connection. She would see him differently, and he wasn't sure he could bear that.

She'd realize that he was a monster.

If she knew why he needed this, connected his past with his sadistic sexual tendencies, she'd walk away. If she did, there would be no getting her back.

Damn it.

Get out of your own head, and back in the scene.

Daniel turned his attention to the bag of toys, shoving the sick feeling of dread deep down inside, boxing it up in a dark corner.

She'd said she needed to scene. Well, so did he. He needed to be in control, and this was the only place he released the bonds on that desperate need. He also needed to spank her, to play with her in ways that caused pleasure, yes…but also pain.

And the root of that need…that was what made him a monster.

CHAPTER 12

"DP—double penetration—via plug, nipple clamps, possibly a clit clamp...though I have other plans for your clit. And some light bondage." Daniel turned from the bag, which he'd put on the chair so he could rummage through it, and held up a shiny pair of clamps and a butt plug.

He wasn't smiling, and for a moment she was worried, because the look on his face was stark. He studied her, then relaxed.

"Worried?" Now the smile was back, and he wiggled the butt plug.

"Oh, absolutely," she breathed.

"Good." His grin melted away to be replaced by intense focus. The way he was looking at her made her pussy and anus clench.

"Hold this for a moment." He passed her the butt plug, which she accepted gingerly.

Her eyes widened when she realized how heavy it was. "Oh, it's solid metal."

"All the better to transfer vibrations, my dear."

He was rummaging in the bag, so she took a moment to

study the plug. It was the classic egg shape, with a nice narrow tip. The neck of the plug was as thick as her thumb, but the base of it, instead of being flat, was a large open circle, big enough for rope to be threaded through, or for two fingers to slide inside. Basically, once it was in he'd have a handy anchor point coming out of her ass.

Damn it, that was hot.

The snap of a glove made her look up. Daniel had two black medical gloves on. He picked up a small packet of lube, ripped the top off with his teeth, and then drizzled the lube onto his fingers.

Her back passage clenched again, and she was hyper aware of her nipples, of the feeling of the air passing over her lower lip with each breath she took.

"On your knees on the blanket. I want your head and shoulders on the ground, ass up."

Pure arousal stabbed through her. The casual way he ordered her to debase herself, to make herself vulnerable so he could play with her intimate parts, was so fucking hot.

Plug in one hand, she moved over onto the blanket he'd spread out, turned so her back was to him.

She knelt, one knee against the side of the Sybian, and the touch of the cold, smooth vinyl made her long to feel it between her legs. She wanted to ride it. Wanted the hard, fast orgasm she knew it could give her.

She very much doubted she'd be allowed to stop with one orgasm, but worrying about having too many orgasms, about how he'd demand she give him everything and then more, wouldn't help her stay calm and obedient for this next part.

Autumn lowered her upper body, folding one arm and pillowing her face on her wrist. The other hand—the one holding the plug—she stretched out to the side, turned so that her palm was up, the toy held loosely. An offering. A signal of how ready she was.

He wasn't gentle with her.

One moment she felt him kneel behind her, one of his legs between her calves, and the next he'd splayed her buttocks and forced the tip of one finger into her. The penetration was shocking and sudden. She cried out, surging forward, away from the sudden intruder.

He didn't let her get away, moved with her so that the tip of his finger was still firmly embedded inside her.

"Surprised you, didn't I?" He ran his other hand over her back, the caress not nearly as smooth as previous ones had been thanks to the glove.

"Yes, Sir."

"Did it hurt?"

"A little."

"And did you like that it hurt, slut?"

She bit her lip, hard enough to make it ache, then released it to reply. "Yes, Sir."

In the same cool, precise tone he said, "And this is what whores like you get, isn't it?" He shoved his finger in deeper.

She cried out, toes curling, ass aching as he forced her tight sphincter open.

"No, no, pet. Bring your ass back here."

She hadn't even realized she'd shifted forward, away from him, until he said something.

With a whimper she rocked back.

"Very good. If you can stay very still, I'll let you have two fingers up your ass before I make you take the plug." He twisted his finger inside her as he spoke.

The sensitive nerve endings in her ass all lit up, sending a confusing signal of mixed pleasure and pain. Her nipples, just barely grazing the rough wool of the blanket, were tight, and knowing they would soon be pinched by clamps was only heightening her arousal.

"What do you say, pet?"

"Thank you, Sir."

"Be specific. I want to hear the words."

"Thank you for preparing my ass with two fingers before you put the plug in me, Sir."

"You're welcome." His finger withdrew, and she heard another packet open.

Cool, thick lube was rubbed over her anus and the surrounding skin. His fingertip penetrated her once more, but this time he didn't just thrust it in. He worked his hand in a circle, pulling and pushing against her anus. After only a few moments of that, she felt the blunt tip of another invader. It was too much, she wasn't ready. Wasn't loose enough to take another finger up the ass.

Daniel shoved, and the tip of the second finger penetrated her. Sweet, hot pain burned at her ass, but she didn't cry out. She only whimpered, a soft sound she repeated with each exhale.

"That's a good whore, taking two fingers up the ass." He pushed them in deeper and her whimpers grew louder.

Her skin felt too sensitive, her body both hot and cold. Her pussy was maddeningly empty. She needed him to fill her there too. Needed him to grab her breasts and scrub her nipples against the blanket. Needed his hand or cock in her mouth.

"Please, please," she moaned.

"That's right." His breathing was labored, and she realized he wasn't unaffected. Touching her, using her, was arousing him, making even his formidable control tremble.

That was so damn sexy.

A disinterested, or bored, partner was horrible. She'd lived through that, and it had...broken her. No. Not broken. Wounded.

Because wounds healed.

And Daniel's touch and words, as harsh as they were,

smoothed her ragged edges, coaxed the torn pieces of her soul back together.

The Doms she normally gravitated towards were those whose control was locked tight, their focus and command of themselves, her, and the scene, absolute. She knew they weren't bored, or unaffected, because with a good Dom she could feel their attention and focus. Doms never ignored her during a scene, unless that was very specifically part of the setup—such as being tied up and put on display. But even then, their lack of attention was usually an act, and she could trust that if she showed any fatigue or discomfort the top would notice and check in.

With Daniel, it was different. He didn't hide how affected he was by her, by their scene.

She wasn't lonely.

Before she could examine that revelation and parse it out, Daniel's fingers withdrew from her ass.

The loss, the emptiness, made her cry out softly, but it didn't last.

"Relax your ass. You're going to take this heavy plug for me, pet."

"Yes, Sir."

When the metal touched her sphincter she cried out, because it was so cold that for a split second it felt hot. In the next moment the coolness of the metal soothed her inflamed, stretched flesh.

He held it there for a moment, long enough that she started to tense up in anticipation. She forced herself to relax by taking deep breaths.

Daniel waited for her to inhale, then forced the plug in. The whole thing slid into her in one shocking penetration. Her ass reflectively clenched the moment the widest part passed through, and the feel of the unforgiving, cold metal stretching her open sent a masochistic thrill through her that made her already throbbing pussy clench.

"What a good whore," Daniel murmured. She heard him remove his gloves and then one bare hand stroked her rump. "You took that plug all at once."

"You didn't give me much of a choice, Sir."

"I didn't, did I?" He tugged on the plug.

The residual pleasure-pain from the abrupt penetration had overshadowed the more subtle feeling of fullness, at least until he started playing with it.

Plugs were diabolical, because they were almost impossible to ignore. The fact that he was playing with the plug pushed that from almost to fully impossible to ignore. At one point he pulled hard enough that she rocked back, and her anus started to open. She thought maybe he would extract and then reinsert it, but instead he held it there, at the point where she was starting to stretch, where the feelings of fullness and pressure were most pronounced.

Then he released it, and her body drew the plug back in, her anus fluttering around the narrow metal neck. Next he twisted it inside her, the circle ring that served as the base rubbing against her ass cheeks as he played with it.

He seemed content to just play with the plug, but she was not.

She needed more. Pleasure or pain, she'd accept either from him, as long as he did *something*. Having her ass played with was delicious, both because it was stimulating the soft nerve endings of her ass and because this checked so many of her submissive desire boxes.

She was on her knees, helpless, being used. He'd inserted a toy into her ass, and was perversely playing with it rather than just fucking her with it.

"Needy slut," Daniel murmured, his voice thick with desire. "Trying to fuck yourself on the plug."

She hadn't realized she was rocking back and forth, working her ass on the plug. She stilled, whimpering in frustration.

"Such a good sub, knowing she should hold still so her master can use her."

Her master. Yes, that felt right.

"If you can hold still for thirty seconds, I'll let you get on the saddle."

Autumn lifted her head and looked back at him, able to see him only out of the corner of her eye. She raised her eyebrows, earning a comically evil chuckle from him.

"Bwah, ha, ha. Yes, you know that I won't make this easy for you."

"Of course not, Sir."

"Time starts when you get back in your proper position." A hard slap to her ass had her dropping back down. As she did her nipples rubbed on the blanket, and it was enough to make her groan, her toes curl.

"What felt good?" Daniel asked.

"My nipples touched the blanket, Sir."

"I have plans for those nipples."

Rather than reply, Autumn focused on locking her muscles, even digging her toes into the blanket.

Then she started to count.

One one thousand, two one thousand.

Plastic snapped. He'd put on another glove.

Four one thousand, five one thousand.

Fingers brushed her pussy, a glancing touch to her labia only, but it was enough to have her sucking in air even as she tightened all her muscles to keep herself still.

"Your cunt is so wet."

Normally she hated the word cunt, but not when he said it. Not when he paired the words with a second soft stroke of his fingers down the seam of her vulva.

Eleven…ish one thousand. She'd lost count.

He opened her pussy, separating the lips so cool air touched the heated core of her sex.

One gloved finger played with her inner labia, flicking and pinching them. The urge to shove back clawed at her. If she did, his finger would slide into her. She'd get the penetration she so desperately needed.

But he'd ordered her to stay still for thirty seconds. She gripped the blanket tighter with her toes and tensed every muscle, her jaw aching.

It was hopeless, because the instant his finger slid down to her clit, circling it with a quick little swirl, she jerked and cried out. She was so aroused that the simple touch felt like he'd touched a live wire to her.

Relief at finally, finally having some pleasure was quickly followed by alarm.

"Damn it," she groaned.

"You lasted longer than I thought." Daniel slid an arm under her, used it to lift her upper body off the blanket. She straightened, but that wasn't enough, because his arm tightened, jerking her off balance so she tipped into him, her back against his chest.

"My patience is almost gone," he growled in her ear. His hands gripped her wrists. He was still wearing a glove and she could feel the one damp finger. Damp because it had been in her wet pussy.

"Use me," she whispered. "However you want. Anything you want."

He forced her arms up, placing them behind his head. She laced her fingers through his hair, body arched to accommodate the position.

He brought his hands together in front of her to strip off the glove, throwing it to the side before cupping her breasts.

As with the touch to her clit, it was a sweet relief when he finally grabbed her breasts. He cupped them, pinching her nipples between his thumb and the side of his knuckle.

She tightened her hands in his hair, arching into the sweet pain.

His head lowered to her neck, and she felt him take a deep breath.

"Autumn…"

She couldn't fully hear him, his word was muffled by her hair, but she was pretty sure he'd said her name. She froze, heart pounding in her chest. He'd said her name like a benediction, with reverence and a need that had nothing to do with sex.

His fingers tightened, compressing her nipples so hard that they turned white and she screamed in pain.

"Did that hurt, slut?" Now his voice was clear, his head no longer buried against her.

"Yesss, Sir."

"Good." He released her breasts to grab her wrists, tugging her hands free of his hair so he could move away.

She didn't want to let go, didn't want to lose the full torso connection between them. Autumn protested with a moan of disappointment when he abandoned her. She shivered as cool air hit her bare back, which had become used to the heat of his body.

He tugged her hair, not hard, but almost reassuringly. She turned to watch as he went to the bag, finally taking out an accessory for the Sybian.

She swiveled on her knees to watch as he first screwed in the small metal penetration piece, then fitted the silicone accessory over the whole top of the saddle, covering the raised ridge and encasing the metal shaft. The long flat panel that lay over the ridge was studded with small bumps. The penetration piece wasn't a dildo, but instead a four-inch tall mushroom-shaped protrusion. Daniel adjusted the angle of the insertable, stepped back to eye it, and then picked up the controller. He studied it, a little smile playing over his lips.

The Sybian kicked on, the motor rumbling to life. It was louder than she remembered.

Daniel pushed something on the remote, and the ridge down the center started to vibrate, the little nubs going blurry with the force of the vibrations.

Daniel laughed, and she glanced over to see that he was looking at her.

"Your eyes are so big right now."

"I don't remember it being that loud or that..." She waved her hand at it in a vague way.

"Intimidating?" He quirked a brow. "No, you're not intimidated by this. You're a little nervous, but you're also aroused."

Autumn snorted. "Thank you, Captain Obvious."

Daniel's eyes narrowed, and the Sybian stopped vibrating.

"Captain Obvious, *Sir*."

The vibrator turned back on.

"Now watch this."

He sounded so enthusiastic, that she couldn't help but smile. Then her stupid heart clenched, a tender feeling softening the sharp, hot edge of her arousal.

That feeling didn't last, because the Sybian made an odd noise, and then the dildo piece started to move. It wasn't just vibrating. It was *rotating*.

Canted at an angle, the fat head was making a roughly 4 inch circle.

"Holy shit," Autumn breathed.

Daniel turned everything off, adjusted the angle of the mushroom dildo, and then set down the controller.

He held out a hand. "Saddle up, lover."

CHAPTER 13

The pet name gave her pause. She stopped, her hand inches from his. Their gazes meet, held.

Daniel's brow furrowed for a moment, but then he closed the distance, grabbing her fingers and tugging her to her feet. He stepped into her personal space, and for a breathless moment she thought he'd kiss her.

She wanted him to kiss her.

She wanted to kiss him.

Instead, Daniel nudged her back a half step with his body, hips bumping hers. The long hard ridge of his cock—straining the laces of his leather—leading the way.

Autumn couldn't help herself, she braced the balls of her feet and leaned into him, grinding her belly against his erection.

Daniel growled low in his throat, then slid his shoe between her ankles. He hooked his foot around one heel and jerked her foot out from under her. She'd guessed that was what he was going to do, so had most of her weight on the other foot, but still, she wobbled and would have had to take a few stumbling steps to catch herself if he hadn't wrapped his arms around her, holding her against his chest.

That was what she'd wanted. Autumn lay her head on his shoulder, rubbing her cheek against the bare skin, hating the tank top that hid some of him.

"Don't try me right now," Daniel murmured in her ear. "My patience is very close to being used up."

"Your patience or your control?"

His arms tightened around her. "Never doubt my control."

There was real anger in his words. She winced. Accusing a dominant of losing control was a terrible idea.

"I didn't mean—"

He grabbed her arms and jerked her away from him.

"I'm sorry—"

"Get on the saddle."

"Daniel."

He froze, glanced at her. There was real anger, and maybe some hurt, in his expression.

"I'm sorry. I didn't mean to say that you aren't in control. For me…for me, knowing my partner is as affected as I am is really important."

He nodded, the line between his brows smoothing.

"Maintaining control is important to me," he said after a moment. He touched her chin. "I want to know more about why it's important to you." He leaned in, kissed her forehead. "Later, we're going to talk."

"All right."

He released her and stepped back. Then kept backing up all the way until his legs hit the chair. Shoving the bag out of his way, he sat.

The gas powered torches and landscape lighting left him in shadow, while the blanket where she was standing, and where the Sybian sat, were comparatively well lit. He was a dark outline, a powerful, hidden man who controlled her…treasured her.

Called her slut and whore, but made her feel beloved. Called her "lover."

"On the saddle," he commanded.

With a submissive nod, she obeyed, stepping over to straddle it, then sinking to her knees.

The mushroom dildo—as she was now calling it in her head—bumped against the plug and she hissed in reaction to the unexpected stimulus.

"Lift your arms. Fingers behind your head the way you had them before."

She glanced up, mouth opening to protest that she needed her arms, needed to brace herself in order to work the mushroom shaped dildo into her vagina.

He caught her gaze, raising a brow while a slight smile played on his lips. He knew exactly what he was asking her to do, and how difficult it would be.

Autumn raised her arms, thighs muscles tensed to keep her balance.

"Oh, and one more thing."

Daniel slid down off the bench, kneeling on the blanket facing her. "You are going to tell me what you're doing. I won't be able to see it when the attachment slips into your pussy, so you'll tell me."

"Yes, Sir."

Controller in hand, he returned to the bench, but this time stayed leaning forward, elbows on his knees.

"Work your cunt onto the toy," he commanded.

Autumn leaned forward and wiggled her hips until she felt the blunt tip. Slowly, so she wouldn't lose her balance, she rubbed her pussy against it, until the rounded head was between her labia. She rose, enough that she could rub her clit against it a few times. She nearly came, and quickly stopped herself, canting her pelvis so the toy slid up the wet valley of her pussy to her entrance.

"You forgot what you were supposed to be doing," he admonished.

"I'm sorry, Sir."

"You were holding your breath a second ago. Why? Pain? Pleasure?"

She could lie to him, but she wouldn't. He deserved the truth. "I rubbed my clit against the dildo."

He reached into the bag. "And is that what I told you to do? Did I tell you to play with your little clit?"

"No, Sir."

He raised a pair of nipple clamps, letting them dangle from his finger. "I'll give you one more chance to follow instructions. Either you start telling me exactly what you're doing, or instead of these clamps, which I intend to screw on nice and tight, I'll go get some clover clamps."

She winced. Clover clamps tightened when the connecting chain was pulled. Even on first application they were painful. While she was masochistic, that level of severe pain didn't fit her mood, or this scene. This was about dominance, obedience, and pleasure.

"I have the mushroom dildo positioned right at...right where it's about to go in."

"The mushroom...?"

"It's sort of shaped like a mushroom."

"Makes sense. It's actually a 'knob stimulator' since it's shaped a bit like a doorknob."

"In that case, the knob is almost inside me." She pursed her lips and rolled her eyes a little at the lame double entendre.

Daniel smiled at her. Reaching out one long arm he stroked the top of her breast, and then flicked her nipple.

"Fuck yourself on it," he said softly. "It's going to be big. And with the plug in your ass, you're going to have to work yourself onto the dildo."

"Yes, Sir." She adjusted her legs one at a time and then sank down. The knob felt impossibly big and blunt. She looked up. "I'm not sure it will fit."

"It will."

She bore down, wiggling. She felt stretched and tight, the plug in her ass shifting with each breath.

Once more Daniel knelt in front of her. "Do you need help?"

"Yes, please." She started to rise up, assuming he was going to reach under her and fuck her with his fingers, or maybe lube up the knob.

"No." Daniel put his hand on her shoulder, arresting her movement.

Holding her gaze, he looped the nipple clamp chain around his neck like a stethoscope and then reached out to pinch and pluck her nipples. Pleasure rippled through her.

He captured the tips of her breasts between thumbs and middle fingers, pinching lightly, and then stroked the flat tip of each nipple with the pad of his index finger. The sensation was so acute that her pussy clenched in reaction to the pleasure, and she moaned, grabbing fistfuls of her own hair and tugging, adding a little bit of pain.

"Talk," he commanded.

"That feels so good. So fucking good. So…so precise. It's like there's a direct line, or nerve, or something, connecting my nipples and clit."

"Good, slut. What else?"

"I'm pulling my hair, because I like it. Because I like that kind of pain." Autumn had closed her eyes, because it was easier to narrate what she was feeling without knowing he was looking at her.

"And your pussy?"

"I'm…I'm wetter now. You made me wetter." She wiggled, rubbing her opening all over the knob. "I'm going to try—"

She stopped on a shriek of pleasure. When she'd shifted her

weight, the knob had slipped inside her with an almost popping sensation.

"It's…it's in," she stammered. Opening her eyes, she met his gaze. "It's big, and with the plug…I feel full."

"Good. Now take it deeper."

She whimpered.

He stroked her cheek. "Take it deeper for me."

She felt soft and helpless. With a whimper she obeyed, working herself down on the knob. It wasn't very long and after only a moment her crotch touched the Sybian.

"Well done. You deserve a reward." Daniel bent his head, taking one of her nipples in his lips. He sucked, tugging her flesh deeper into the warm, wet hollow of his mouth.

She moaned, and arched into his face, which changed the angle of her hips, the knob sliding in a little bit more, while the ring handle of the plug came to rest on the saddle.

He switched to her other nipple, his finger going to the first, pinching and pulling, until the saliva-damp skin slid from between his fingers.

Autumn closed her eyes, whimpering in submissive bliss. She felt full and used, pleasured and owned. His forcing her—with nothing more than his words, his dominance—to take the thick toy in her pussy had pushed a button she hadn't known she had. She loved this feeling of being forced to participate in her own degradation, of him commanding her to continue even when it seemed to be too much. Ordering her to fuck herself on the machine, while her ass was already plugged and sore from the spanking.

He pulled back, her nipple slipping from his mouth with an audible pop. She watched with soft, wary eyes as he slid the clamps from around his neck.

The first one went on the nipple he'd been fingering, rubber-coated teeth biting down on her flesh. When he used the screw to tighten the jaws she cried out, looking up at him, pleading without words for mercy.

He tightened it further.

Her head dropped in submissive acceptance as pain shivered down her torso. The other clamp went on just as tight, and she was making a soft, whimpering, whining sound at the back of her throat by the time he finished.

"You're beautiful like this."

"Will you tell me? What…what you see?" she asked haltingly.

His gaze searched her face. "Yes, lover, I will. But first, I think you've earned a reward."

He picked up the controller.

A second later the motors between her thighs hummed to life, though the attachment was still.

"Lean forward a bit, so your clit is making contact."

The moment she'd obeyed, adjusting the angle of her hips by arching her back, rather than actually leaning forward, which would probably cause her to faceplant, he flipped on the vibration.

Half a dozen soft little nubs were pressed into her clit and the surrounding skin. Each one of those started to vibrate.

"Holy shit," Autumn breathed.

"How does it feel?"

"So…so good. Oh god it's so, so good…I—"

The orgasm took her by surprise. Between one breath and the next the pleasure and pain he'd given her and the submission he'd demanded from her, came together with the pure physical stimulation of her clit. It was an orgasm built not just of physical sensation, but of emotional and mental pleasure.

Autumn reared back, screaming with the force of her orgasm. Her hands fell from her hair, slamming down onto the saddle, elbows locked to keep herself upright.

The vibrations slowed, and her orgasm started to subside. She was shaking, shivering.

That's when he turned on the knob.

Deep in her pussy, the rounded invader started to move, swirling in a small circle. It was unlike anything she'd ever felt before, a strange, invasive, demanding touch. The kind of thing only a Dom, her Dom, who felt it was his right to touch and use every part of her body, would ever have dared. Each rotation made the fat head slide over her G-spot, then as it rotated to the back, bump against the plug.

Soon she was rocking in time with the rhythm, her body, which should have been replete after that first orgasm, starting to tighten once more.

"Please," she whimpered.

"Please stop?" He waited, but all she could do was moan and rock her hips, fucking herself on the machine. "Please give you more?"

She shook her head, not in denial, but because she wasn't sure what she was asking for.

"Luckily," he murmured, "it's not your decision to make, is it?"

"No, Sir."

He flicked something, and the vibrations started up again. This time not only was the area below her clit vibrating, but so was the rear section. The base of the plug, wedged against the machine, transmitted those vibrations to her ass. The tender, surprisingly sensitive nerves of her ass hummed in response to the stimulation.

Daniel stood and started tearing at the laces of his leathers.

Autumn licked her lips, staring hungrily at his crotch. He'd filled both her ass and pussy, trapped her clit against the vibrating nubs, and clamped her nipples. The final thing she needed was something in her mouth. His cock in her mouth.

Shoving his pants down to his hips he shuffled forward.

Without waiting for the command, she reached out, grasping his dick and bringing it towards her open mouth.

Daniel slapped her hand away. Looking up, she was shocked to see that he looked angry.

"No. We had an agreement."

"But..." Everything had changed since then. She'd shared more with him, felt more, in these few hours, than she had in months of relationships with other men.

Daniel's eyes glittered as he reached down, grabbing the chain between the clamps. He lifted it and thrust it between her teeth.

"Bite," he commanded with a snap.

She closed her teeth around the chain, felt the tug as the clamps lifted, torquing her nipples.

"I will not break my word to you. Not ever. Do you understand?" He stroked her cheek with the back of his fingers.

She nodded, very carefully.

Daniel smiled down at her, the expression changing to something dark and dominant as his gaze slid down her body.

He stooped, grabbing the controller, then rose again, his cock so hard that it was angled up towards the sky.

"Use your hands on me," he demanded.

Between her legs, the vibrations increased.

"I know you're sensitive. Sensitive enough that the Sybian is causing you pleasure that is almost pain. That will only get worse."

He was right. Her clit, still sensitive from her last orgasm sent conflicting signals to her brain—pleasure, pain. It distilled to simple sensation.

"I'll turn it off when you make me come."

Autumn reached to the side, grasping his cock in one fist, the other hand teasing his sensitive head, circling it with her fingers.

That motion echoed the way the knob was swirling inside her, hitting her g-spot with each pass.

"Lift your chin for me," he murmured as he thrust into her hand.

She obeyed, whining around the chain clamped between her teeth as her nipples started to burn from sweet pain.

"Fuck, I'm close," he murmured.

She cupped her palm over the tip of his cock, her hand slick from the fluid leaking from the slit. If she hadn't had the chain between her teeth she wouldn't have been able to stop herself from taking a taste.

Another orgasm ripped through her, and she wasn't sure what was the catalyst—her clit being vibrated, the knob whirling inside her, the plug up her ass, or the sweet burning of her nipples thanks to the clamps.

Or maybe it was him. Knowing that topping her had brought him so close to his own release, despite the relatively little physical stimulus he'd had.

"Autumn."

Her name was a command, and a prayer.

"Look up."

Hand working his cock, she looked up at him, straining to do it without moving her head.

"No. Raise your chin and look at me."

Something inside her relaxed, even as her body began to tighten once more as she approached another shattering orgasm.

She raised her chin, meeting his gaze. He'd commanded her to look up, knowing that it would mean added pain from the clamps. And she obeyed because he'd ordered her to. Because she trusted him enough to obey without worrying he hadn't thought it through, or didn't realize what he was asking. He knew. He wanted her to have that pain.

They looked into one another's eyes, and everything faded

away, the murmur of conversation coming from the other people in the courtyard, the buzz of the machine between her legs. It was just them, two people caught up in a moment of synchrony, their wants and needs meshing together so well that it was like an endless feedback loop.

The clamps, not tight enough to hold when forced to bear the weight of her breasts, popped off. Autumn's eyes widened, and she screamed, not just in pain, but in pleasure, as the unexpected removal of the clamps trigged her third, blistering orgasm.

Daniel groaned, thrusting hard into her hands, the head of his cock grinding against her palm before he coated her fingers with ejaculate.

She hung there, caught in a pleasure so great that her muscles cramped and her ears were ringing.

Then the wave broke, the pleasure fading like water drawn back out to sea.

But the Sybian was still buzzing away. Her whole body felt like the skin had been stripped away, her nerves exposed. The pain she felt was no longer pleasure-pain, but pure over-stimulation. She opened her mouth, the chain of the clamps falling out.

"Daniel," she gasped.

"I've got you, I've got you." The Sybian clicked off, and then he was there, kneeling beside her, hugging her close as he eased her up and off the knob.

"Relax, lover, I've got you. Just hold on to me."

She whimpered into his shoulder as he reached around and removed the plug, her ass spasming. Her whole lower body still buzzed faintly, leftover sensation from being astride something that vibrated.

Daniel sat back, legs stretched out in front of him, spread enough so that he could nestle her between his thighs. He'd pulled up his leathers at some point, but hadn't re-laced them. She could feel his still semi-hard cock against her ass.

He must have signaled someone for help, because a moment later he was handed a soft blanket, not one of the wool ones from the courtyard basket. He draped it over her, pulling it up to her chin. She snuggled against his chest and closed her eyes.

She felt his lips touch the top of her head, a soft, barely-there kiss.

"You were beautiful, perfect," he murmured. "Just rest now. Let me take care of you."

She was glad he couldn't see her face, didn't see the silent tears that slid from under her lashes. If he'd asked why she was crying, she wouldn't have been able to give him an answer.

CHAPTER 14

Daniel kept his arm around her as they walked back to the library. It was called the library, but the lovely dark wood shelves held collections of antique sex toys rather than books. It also had a long bar against one wall. The club was hopping, as full as he'd ever seen it. Every barstool was occupied, as were the several small cocktail tables near it, and the large couches by the mission-style fireplace.

"Hold on, just wait here for a second," he murmured to her.

She nodded, her heavy-lidded eyes focused on the middle distance.

He snagged an empty club chair—with permission from the Dom sitting in its mate. The chair's former occupant was no doubt the woman currently kneeling on the floor with her head bent.

Dragging the chair into a corner, he half turned it so that they were facing one of the bookshelf walls but could still see the room. He wanted some privacy.

The lighted display in the closest bookcase was a series of glass dildos in graduated sizes. They caught the light, refracting it beautifully.

Daniel collected Autumn, wrapping his arms around her once more and guiding her through the room. A few Doms nodded at him, a brief acknowledgment. Every person in there knew, based not just on the blanket, but by the way he had his arm around her, his head bent over hers, that they were post-scene and about to engage in some aftercare.

When they reached the chair, he sat then tugged her down onto his lap so her back was to the room. She sat gingerly, wincing a little. If he were a truly good and chivalrous man her wince would have made him feel guilty. Instead he felt satisfied.

Spreading his knees, he shifted her so that her ass was between his knees, her legs draped over one thigh, her back supported by both his arm and the curved armrest of the chair. She wiggled, scooting herself further down so that she could rest her head against his neck and cheek.

"How are you feeling?"

She took her time answering. He stroked her leg over the blanket, ready to be patient, to sit in silence, for as long as she needed.

"Tired. Sore." Her voice was a little scratchy.

"If you give me a second, I'll get up and get you some more water."

In the immediate aftermath of the scene he'd given her a water bottle, which she'd chugged while he cleaned her hand and then between her ass cheeks, with baby wipes.

"I'd rather you stay here," she murmured.

"All right, lover." The endearment came out of his mouth before he'd thought through the reasons why he shouldn't say it.

Autumn tensed in his arms, then shifted, pushing herself up enough that she could twist to face him.

"You called me that before, in the scene."

His heart was hammering in his chest and there were butterflies in his stomach. He was fucking ridiculous. He hadn't felt like this since…well, he didn't remember. If he were a normal person it would have been some cute story, like he'd felt these flutters the first time he kissed someone. But he wasn't normal, and there were no cute stories.

"I did."

Her eyes scanned his face, feature by feature. "You didn't call me pet, or slut, or whore."

"I think I called you all those things." He leered, and she smiled, which was the effect he'd been hoping for.

"You did, but not towards the end. Even though what I was doing…what you were making me do…was objectively whore-y."

"Whore-y."

"There really isn't a better word to describe being fucked by a machine with a plug in your ass, nipple clamps on, while also jerking off a hot guy." She arched a brow, as if daring him to correct that statement.

He grinned. Damn, he liked talking to her. "There's an argument to be made that you were just being a good submissive."

"I am a terrible submissive."

"No." He caught one of her hands, lacing their fingers together. "You're not a terrible submissive."

She looked away, gaze scanning the room, then whispered something so low he couldn't hear it. It sounded like "Not for you." but he couldn't be sure.

"Autumn, talk to me." He stroked her cheek.

"Why?" She faced him once more. "Wait, I don't mean why should I talk to you." She took a breath, and when that caused the blanket to slip down her shoulders she didn't stop it.

Daniel reached out, grabbing the fabric and tugging it up around her neck.

"Why did you stop using those words? After all, it was part of our checklist assignment."

It hadn't been a conscious choice, but the minute she asked

the question, he knew the answer. And from the look on her face, he suspected that she knew the answer too.

He stayed silent, waiting for her to verbalize it first.

"It's because you knew... You knew if you called me a whore, or a slut, while I was doing something whore-y, it would hurt."

"Yes." That was true, but it wasn't the full truth.

"How?" she asked.

He shrugged. "Good Dom instincts. Experience. The look on your face. All possibilities."

"We just met, and you realized something they—" She cut herself off.

"Ah, good. We're here. I've been waiting for this part."

"What part?" She'd hunched her shoulders and was no longer looking at him.

"Your sub origin story."

That startled a laugh out of her.

He smiled, relieved that he could make her laugh, could keep her rooted and safe both physically and emotionally.

"My sub origin story." She was grinning.

"Someone hurt you." He ran his hand up her back, slid it under her hair, pulling the dark strands out from under the blanket. "Someone taught you to hate your submissive needs. Did such a number on you, here—" He touched her temple. "—that you were angry at, and secretly scared for, other subs."

Her smile faded, but she didn't retreat into herself.

"I didn't approach it, this, right." She gestured to the club around them. "I tried to add D/s to a vanilla relationship."

"Your boyfriend wasn't into it, and made you feel bad? Called you names."

"Not the first one, that was the second one. And yes, like a dumbass I tried it twice. After that, I learned."

"So what did the first one do?" He kept his tone light, fighting to hide the rage he was feeling towards these unnamed men who had dared to hurt his lover.

Emphasis on *his*. He was feeling seriously possessive.

"He was willing to try. He spanked me, used a plug, a little bondage, but he wasn't into it."

That wasn't what he'd been expecting.

"He would...he would lose his erection halfway through the scene. He'd ask me exactly what I wanted. He'd do things wrong, not on purpose, but just because he wasn't thinking about it...didn't care enough to have planned or read anything. Maybe if I'd taken us to munches, or demos at clubs..."

She took a shaky breath, and he tugged her closer, pressing a lingering kiss to her temple. He felt sad for the woman she'd been, who'd opened herself up to a partner, exposed something raw and vulnerable only to have it fall flat.

"I could just tell it was a chore for him. That his mind was usually elsewhere. I mean that was a problem in our relationship from the start. He was brilliant, worked at JPL, but not good at practical stuff. Not good at planning and executing non-academic things."

"So you had to play both parts in the scenes. The Dom and sub."

"I'd always thought of it as being forced to top from the bottom, but...you're right. I really was the Dom." She was quiet for a moment. "I remember this one time I was just in the mood, you know? I don't even remember why. Maybe I'd read a sexy book, or seen something hot, but I *needed* him."

"Needed to scene with a Dom," he countered.

"Probably more accurate." Autumn snuggled against him. "I put on lingerie—one of those strappy harnesses, no underwear, and a robe. Not a fluffy robe, a sheer black one. Totally see through. I lay on the bed, and just waited. By the time he came in I was so fucking turned on. In my head I could pretend that the waiting was the first part of the scene. That he was making me wait so I'd be ready."

Daniel's imagination painted a vivid picture of her like that, but in his mind the bed she was on was his. "Then he walked in, put you on your knees, spanked you, fucked you from behind but didn't let you come. Then he spread you out on the bed. Tied you down so you were helpless, and played with you for hours."

"Is that what you'd have done?" she asked in a small voice.

"It would be a good start."

"If that had happened, I'd probably still be with him."

"So what did he do?"

"He looked at me, said 'oh, I see' in this sort of irritating demeaning way, though I don't think he meant it like that. Then he decided to go turn off all the lights, make sure his cat was inside, brush his teeth...basically get ready for bed. I mean he was doing it quicker than normal, but I just...I felt so *stupid*."

"I'm so sorry, lover." He rubbed his lips against her hair.

"It's dumb, because I mean, getting ready for bed made sense, right?"

"No. Getting ready for bed is what you do on a normal night. You were very clearly signaling that you wanted something different on that particular night. You were changing it up, and he should have done the same."

"That's...that's a really good point." Autumn sat up straight, eyes narrowed though she was staring into middle distance. "It *wasn't* too much to expect him to get with it and feed the cat after he fucked me."

"Perfectly reasonable." He slid his fingers through her hair, gently massaging her scalp. "You needed something that night, and he didn't take care of you."

"He tried. I mean I know he tried. He went for the toy box, but then couldn't find the lube, stopped and asked if he could use a bottle of massage oil that was in there. I said sure, but he googled to check. I offered to give him head to get us started, which worked, but then when I was in position for a spanking I look over and his dick had gone soft. I was…I was a chore to him."

Her voice was tight, and she was blinking fast. Daniel kissed her shoulder, fighting the urge to turn her over his knee so that when he was done she'd get to see exactly how hard spanking her made him.

"It wasn't…malicious. He just wasn't into it. And he tried, but the fact that he so clearly didn't enjoy it was…" She looked at him, smiling tentatively. "It was so hot when I could tell that you were into it. That you were having to fight to control yourself."

"How could I not? You're delicious." He touched her skin with the tip of his tongue.

Her eyes were bright, her breathing uneven.

"Tell me about the other one," he murmured.

She jumped, as if he'd shocked her. He considered saying she didn't have to, that it didn't matter, but he knew it did. And if he was going to be her lover, her top, he needed to know.

"The second time I tried, it was with a guy who was more naturally dominant. Decisive, aggressive even, though in a take-charge kind of way, not the start-a-bar fight style aggression."

"Let me guess, he's the one who called you a slut."

"He liked 'dirty talk'." Her lips twisted in a grimace. "He was into the D/s, but when I tried to explain I didn't have a degradation kink, that I didn't like being called those names, he said that they worked for him. Helped him get in the mood."

"Did you set a hard limit for no name-calling?"

"No, because…because I was scared if I did that he wouldn't want to do it at all."

"You were willing to take what you could get, even if it hurt you."

"Yes. For a while. I left when…when he started expecting me to be submissive all the time. Ordered me to kneel while we watched TV. Expected me to answer with a 'Yes, Master' when we were out in public. He bought me a day collar—a very ugly necklace. When I asked if he was fucking joking, he got pissed."

"And that's how you developed a disdain for people like Master Carter and Pet."

"Pretty much. After that I gave up on BDSM. At least until I started making serious money. Then I found out about, and joined, Las Palmas."

She seemed to sink into herself a little after that, but it felt more like it was due to relaxation than a protective physical retreat.

"That's quite the origin story," he said.

"I've never told anyone those things. I mean my girlfriends know a little bit, but they don't know it all. They don't know about Las Palmas either. They think this is some boring club for finance people."

"Is that what you do? Finance stuff?"

She looked at him, then quickly looked away. "I...I don't share that with people here. What I do."

That hurt. It shouldn't, because most people didn't talk about their jobs at the club. Many used fake names as an added layer of protection.

She was watching him warily, as if waiting for him to react badly. Because of that, Daniel made sure his expression didn't change. She relaxed once more. He kept up the head massage, occasionally moving down to knead the muscles of her shoulders and neck.

"Now you know all my secrets," Autumn murmured. "You know that I'm a sub who doesn't respect subs—"

"You're not," he said firmly.

"—and therapy-ed me until I realized that I was scared for them, probably because of how my relationship with Mike ended."

"I was unaware therapy was a verb."

"And what we just did was the best scene I've ever had."

Daniel took a satisfied breath. "I like hearing that."

They sat in silence for a while. She'd shared her origin story…it was only right he do the same.

The words wouldn't come. They sat there in silence. A silence that changed from companionable to tense as the minutes ticked by. Around them people came and went from the library. There were voices interspersed with the cracking sounds of someone getting spanked, and occasional moans of pleasure.

Damn it. Why couldn't he just tell her?

Daniel didn't hide his past, but he also didn't talk about it. Because of what he'd done when he finally got out, there was no way to keep it secret. After all, his congressional testimony was public record.

But if he were to start talking about his past right now, it wouldn't be just the facts of what had happened. It wouldn't be a calm recitation of what he'd been through and how it had affected him. He knew how to tell that story without breaking down, to tell it like he was speaking about someone else, as if who he'd been was a separate person.

Autumn sat up, wiggling until she was perched on his thigh, but with her feet on the floor. "I know we're not done with our letter, but I think I need a few days to recov—"

"What bar?"

She glanced at him, raising a brow "What bar…?"

"What bar would we have met at?" he asked. "Dive bar in Silver Lake? The hotel bar at the Standard on the Sunset Strip?"

Her lips twitched in a smile. "Downtown L.A. One of the themed ones."

"Themed bar?" He shook his head. "Really?"

"Oh yeah. That one in the basement with the old bank vault that's like a speakeasy. Or the hipster one that looks like an old hunting lodge and serves whiskey cocktails. I unapologetically love bars with weird themes and decor."

"In that case I would have been slightly embarrassed to be there."

"Okay, what if I'd met you at one of your favorite bars?" She pursed her lips. "Where would it be?"

"Rooftop garden bar at the Bungalow in Santa Monica."

"Touristy."

"Great view of the ocean."

Autumn shrugged out of the blanket, letting it fall to her waist, but only for a moment. He got a quick glimpse of her pretty breasts, the small marks he'd made easier to see in this light. Then she was pulling the blanket up, under her arms, and tucking it around her like a towel.

"If we had met at that bar, if we had left together, I would never have told you I like to be sexually submissive." She stood, smiling down at him. "We would never have gotten to this."

Daniel had to curl his fingers into fists to stop himself from reaching out and grabbing her, pulling her back down onto his lap. "We aren't done with our letter."

"I know, but..." She raised one brow. "Honestly, I think we more than satisfied the requirements."

"We didn't do nipple weights. And didn't play with your piercings. I have them stored safely, by the way." Daniel stood, which put him solidly in her personal space. Autumn narrowed her eyes and didn't back down. "I'm not done with you, lover."

"Next weekend, then."

"Tomorrow night."

"No. I have plans."

"No, you don't."

"I have plans to not be here."

She raised her chin, as if daring him to challenge the statement.

Their scene had been good. So damned good. He wanted to play with her again tonight—it was early enough, and then again tomorrow.

She was pulling back.

Probably because she shared her past with you, was open and vulnerable, and instead of reciprocating you stonewalled her with silence.

She'd shared things with him. Told him both her dark secret and how previous relationships had shaped her kink.

He hadn't been brave enough to do either. Damn.

He could explain that he didn't talk about his past, not at Las Palmas. He could encourage her to stay, pull her back onto his lap, and touch her, gently at first, but with increasing intimacy, until she was ready to go again.

There was something in the tightness of the skin around her eyes that stopped him.

"Next weekend." Daniel stepped back, out of her space.

She relaxed. "Thank you. For listening. For making me feel… a little less broken."

"You were never broken," he assured her.

"Hearing you say it makes me believe it just a little bit more." She gathered her long blanket train, holding it in the hand not pressed to her breasts to keep the rest of it in place. "Until next weekend, Sir." She added a sassy little wink.

Daniel watched her walk away, and hated himself for not being brave enough to stop her.

CHAPTER 15

"This is stupid. I'm sorry." Autumn looked at her best friend. "You should go home."

Summer gestured with her glass. "Don't be stupid. I'm your ride-or-die bitch."

"Cheers to that." Autumn picked up her own glass and touched it to Summer's. It wasn't the first time this evening they'd toasted.

They'd been friends since freshman year of college when they'd been roommates. Someone in the housing department thought they were clever, assigning girls named Autumn and Summer to the same room. They'd bonded over a similar feelings about their names—both of them having a combination of irritation and pride in their seasonal names.

They'd held each other's hands through those first awkward months of college. Their lives had taken different, if parallel, tracks in the past few years. They were both finally established in their careers. Summer was going to save humanity from itself. She was a program manager for a major environmental non-profit.

Autumn had always been good with numbers, but earned her

BA in economics, which was an odd major, since economists were people with advanced degrees, and besides that, her best job prospect was to teach.

She'd gone a different route, making her own way in the world of what she liked to think of as fake-money.

Now she was a hedge fund manager, a position she'd taken just because it was a new challenge. They'd begged her to come on board because Autumn had made a name for herself, and an ungodly amount of money, as a day trader. High risk, high reward, and the earning potential had been nearly unlimited.

She'd paid off her parents' house, was paying cash for her siblings' college tuition, and her abuela was still lighting candles for her every week, because she was sure Autumn had to be doing something illegal to have made that much money that fast.

Her day-trading mentor—one of her professors—had always said she had a super high EQ—emotional quotient, to go with a good IQ, which was why she could handle high risk day trading. Before yesterday, she would have agreed with him.

But it had taken Daniel to point out that she didn't actually despise other submissives, but was, in fact, afraid for them. Afraid they'd experience the pain she'd gone through. So much for a high emotional quotient.

"Remind me again who we're looking for?" Summer leaned in, head swiveling so she could scan the crowd in the dim bar with narrowed eyes.

"We're not looking for anyone. He probably won't come. It was just something we said in passing."

With every minute that passed, Autumn felt a little stupider for coming here. The hunting-lodge themed whiskey bar was her local hangout, since her downtown LA condo was up on the twenty-seventh floor of this same building. She'd spent the day in her pajamas, studiously not thinking about Daniel. She'd planned to keep that going right through the night, but as the sun set she'd gotten antsy with the need to do something.

What bar would we have met at?

His question ran on a loop through her brain as she showered, did her hair, and put on her best jeans and a black stretchy top with a deep V and ruched detailing on the sleeves. Jeans and a cute top was the universal going out standard in L.A.

She'd been about to order a car to take her out to Santa Monica when some semblance of sanity returned. She wasn't going to go sit alone in the rooftop bar at the Bungalow, hoping he'd show up. That wasn't romantic, it was somewhere between pathetic and stalker.

Instead she'd called Summer, who'd still been at work in East L.A. Summer jumped on the gold line train and met her upstairs at her condo, where she'd borrowed a cute top to go with the jeans she was already wearing. Then, arm in arm, they'd taken the elevator down to the second floor of the building, passing out of the private residences' lobby and into the small landing where a faux log-cabin door marked the entrance to the bar.

While they sipped their first drink, Autumn had told Summer about Daniel. Not all of it, but enough. She'd met a man at that secret club she belonged to—the one Summer thought was some sort of finance world power broker hangout. They'd hit it off, talked, but not exchanged numbers, because that was frowned upon in the club. Summer had made a weird face at that, but hadn't called her out, so Autumn kept up the lie, saying that though they hadn't exchanged information, she'd told Daniel about her two favorite bars.

Summer had been all for splitting up, one of them going to the other bar which was a few streets over in the basement of what used to be a bank. Now people could sip drinks while sitting in the old vault. Autumn had shut that shit down, because she felt stupid enough already. Having to sit here by herself, while Summer was at the other place, would only make it worse.

"I could send John to the Bungalow."

Summer's fiance had good-naturedly told them to have a fun time and for Summer to call him when she was ready for a ride home.

"How would John know who to look for?" Autumn asked.

"He could take pictures of everyone in the bar and send them to us."

"Well that sounds like a really good way to be super creepy and get thrown out of the bar and possibly arrested."

"Hmm, probably true. Anyway, what does he look like again?"

"Brown hair, light colored eyes. Nice suit. Really sharp, looks very…in control."

"Nice smile?" Summer asked.

"The best smile," Autumn sighed.

"Okay then," Summer picked up her phone and started to scoot out from behind their little table.

"What are you doing?"

"Calling John. There's a sharply dressed man with a killer smile headed this way."

Autumn's heart stopped. She widened her eyes at her friend, who stopped scooting. Summer cast a critical eye over her, then reached out, grabbed the front of Autumn's shirt, and yanked it down several inches. Autumn's cleavage was now fully on display center stage.

"Summer," Autumn hissed.

"Get ready," her friend murmured.

"Hello."

She'd convinced herself, during her pajama-clad lounging, that their chemistry had probably just been a product of the combination of attraction and predisposition towards sexual arousal due to the setting.

But one word, uttered in that wonderful voice, wiped away all the justifications and explanations she'd come up with.

Autumn took a breath and turned in her seat.

Daniel looked elegant and dangerous, when he should have looked stuffy in the three-piece suit. His jacket and the bottom button of his waistcoat were undone, and he had one hand in his pocket, pulling that side of the jacket back.

She looked up, met his gaze, and knew that she was looking into the eyes of a man, maybe the only man, who could make her truly, deeply happy.

The moment seemed to last forever, or maybe time stood still for them.

Summer, grinning like an idiot, finished sliding away—after not so subtly taking a picture of Daniel. "Just in case I need to be able to give the police a lead," she said as she sauntered off.

Daniel's smile widened into a grin. "Friend?"

"Best friend. She came to wait with me."

"Oh? And who were you waiting for?" He held out a hand. "I'm Daniel, by the way."

Ahh, okay. This was how they were doing it. She shook his hand, "Autumn."

"Can I buy you a drink?"

"I have one." She lifted her nearly full glass. "Can I buy you one?"

He didn't balk or look offended or pull any other stupid toxic masculine bullshit. "Yes, thank you."

"What would you like?" Autumn managed to catch the eye of one of the servers.

He ordered a whiskey sour from the server, who headed for the bar, leaving them alone together.

"You know," Daniel said after a moment. "This is the third bar I've been to tonight."

Autumn let out a soft laugh, shaking her head. "That's

funny. I was having trouble deciding which bar I should go to. There were three possibilities."

"Did you go to all of them?"

"No, I thought maybe I should just stay here and wait."

"Shall I do a clichéd pickup line about how you must have been waiting for me?" His words said one thing, but his expression...it was tentative. He wanted to make sure she was here waiting for him.

"No clichés. I think you're...we're better than that."

"You're right. We are."

The server delivered his drink, and Daniel raised it. "A toast."

"What are we toasting to?" She picked up her own glass.

"To...meeting in bars."

They each took a sip, setting their glasses down almost in sync. Daniel scooted over, so he was sitting in the corner of the padded bench area. He stretched his arms out along the top of the bench seating. She thought she felt his fingers brush against her hair, a touch so feather light she couldn't be sure it was real.

No more pretending.

Autumn slid over, cuddling against Daniel's side. His arm dropped down to encircle her. Holding her close.

"Hi," she whispered.

"Hi," he replied, just as quietly.

"I thought it was crazy of me to do this. To come here in case you came looking for me."

"I was going crazy worrying that we'd miss each other by hopping from place to place. It would be like a scene from a movie, I'd walk in minutes after you left."

"We really should have exchanged numbers."

"Maybe, but maybe you weren't ready for that yesterday." He shifted, easing her away enough so that he could look down at her. "Maybe you weren't ready, because you'd opened yourself up. You told me your secret, and about your past." He took a deep breath. "I didn't reciprocate."

She'd expected him to. Had sat quietly on his lap for half an hour, assuming he was going to start talking. The fact that he hadn't shared anything personal with her, after she'd shared so much with him, had hurt, but by that point she'd been emotionally wrung out enough that she hadn't had the energy to get really upset.

But it had made it easier to call a halt to their time together.

"I noticed."

"And I noticed you noticing." He licked his lips, seeming nervous. No, not nervous…wary. "My past, at least within the club, isn't something I talk about."

"'At least within the club'? That sounds a bit ominous."

He looked around, at the bar that was getting louder by the minute as it approached 9p.m. and more people poured in.

"Too loud in here?" she asked.

"No, it will be fine."

"Because I live upstairs." She pointed at the ceiling.

He arched a brow. "Are you inviting me up?"

"Yes."

CHAPTER 16

Twenty minutes later, Daniel watched as she used her thumbprint to unlock her front door. They were in the heart of downtown L.A., so he should have figured that any residence in the high rise would be state of the art. The building was mixed use, and according to the signage, housed two floors of retail and commercial establishments, including the bar, several law offices, as well as design and accounting firms.

An entirely separate bank of elevators serviced the residences, and in the elevator a live security screen showed a guard, who greeted Autumn by name—Ms. Herrera—and then asked for her guest's name.

He'd given it, watched as the guard typed it in. Daniel was pretty damned sure that a still of his face was being catalogued for security records.

When they left the elevator, Daniel cleared his throat. "You know, I've been in high security government buildings that probably had worse security than your elevator."

"It's a bit over the top, but it's nice to know that if I'm ever hideously murdered, they'll have plenty of leads."

She opened the door and lights clicked on automatically. She took off her wrist clutch, placing it on an all glass table by the door.

"Should I be worried that it's the second time tonight someone has taken my picture for a potential Dateline special?"

"If you say 'not all men'…"

"I would never." He followed her from the foyer with its honey wood flooring, white walls, glass table with a green glass key bowl, into a massive open-concept living space. A floor to ceiling glass wall showed a panoramic view of downtown, the buildings creating great steel and glass valleys. Beyond those the city spread, glittering gold and white at night.

Daniel whistled. He was highly successful, and had more money than he'd ever dreamed of, but he could still be impressed. This condo was probably worth as much as his house on the canals in Venice.

"Would you like a glass of wine?" Autumn walked behind the massive kitchen island, which had to be twenty feet long. "Or something stronger?"

"Not yet, I'd like to talk first."

She braced her hands on the counter. "That sounds a little ominous."

He took his suit jacket off, draping it over the back of one of the half dozen chairs that lined the living room side of the island. "I didn't mean it to, but you have the right to hear about my past, and…" He steeled himself. "My secret, before this progresses."

"This." She pressed her lips together, then pushed off the counter. She tapped one of the narrow white panels that covered the wall at the end of the kitchen. It went from opaque to transparent, revealing a massive wine fridge. She pushed on it and the door popped open, allowing her to select a bottle. Reaching into a drawer in the island, she took out a small wood box. He went around the end of the island, and without a word she handed him the box while she went for a glass. As he'd expected, the box held a wine set. He opened her bottle of Riesling. When she set a delicate long-stemmed white wine glass on the counter, he poured her a generous glass, then capped the wine with the stopper from the box.

She led the way to a set of curved chaise lounges positioned to take advantage of the view. Autumn placed her glass on the floor with a click before taking a seat and reaching for the zip on the inside of her gray boots.

Daniel took a knee and unzipped them for her, easing first her boot, and then the thin black socks she wore, off of her feet. He'd seen her barefoot. He'd seen her naked. But there was something very intimate and vulnerable about removing her shoes here in her own home.

Impulsively, he cupped her heel, then leaned down to kiss the top of her foot.

"I thought you wanted to tell me your secrets before this progressed?" Her question was soft, not accusatory.

Daniel released her foot, resting his forehead against her knee. "I did. I'm sorry. I shouldn't have touched you, but..."

"I like it when you touch me. It terrifies me, but..."

She let her words trail off, matching what he said. Her fingers slid through his hair, gently scratching his scalp. If he'd been a cat he would have purred.

"It terrifies me that you're here," she went on. "I promised myself I would never mix the two sides of my life. I tried it, twice. Didn't work. It's why I didn't want to scene with you." Her voice turned wry. "Because you seemed like...whoops, I mean you *are*...the kind of guy I'd bring home from the bar."

"And I'm...a dangerous liar."

Her hand stilled in his hair. Daniel lifted his head from her lap, pushing slowly to his feet and then dropping onto the other chaise.

"What do you mean you're a liar?" Her gaze was hard, sharp.

"Let me clarify. I never told you a lie."

She reached down for her glass, tapping it against her lip before she took a sip.

"I'm a liar because...because this, all of this?" He gestured to himself. "This is all a facade. I dress the part. I have the house. But my past, and my genetics..."

"Seriously?" Autumn's shoulders sagged with relief. "I thought you were going to tell me that you're an undercover federal agent. Not that you suffer from imposter syndrome or have shitty parents."

"I'm sorry, you were worried I was a *what?*" Daniel just stared at her

"An undercover agent."

"In a BDSM club? Why in the world would you think that? Is that even a thing?"

"I maybe read too many Lexi Blake books. Anyway, ignore that. Go on."

He opened his mouth, closed it. Then shook his head. Strangely, that weird little byplay made him feel better.

Right then he knew, just knew, that nothing he could tell her, except, apparently, that he was an undercover agent, would make her think less of him. Though they were so very different, they were the same, both scared to trust, afraid.

"I think I'm falling in love with you." It wasn't what he'd meant to say. He was supposed to be walking her through his fucked up childhood. That didn't seem as important right now as it had when they walked in.

Autumn froze, eyes wide.

"I don't expect you to say anything back. I don't expect... well anything. It just felt important that I tell you."

"You jerk," she breathed, but she was smiling. "I'm working very hard on not falling for you, and you go and say something like that?"

Hope made him smile, but a nasty voice in his head told him that he was wrong. That when he told her about his past, realized where his sadistic tendencies came from, she'd throw him out.

"And before you go any further, you should know that this is new for me, too. I don't come from money. My great-grandparents were migrant workers, and I grew up lower middle class. My grandmother is convinced I must be a criminal—a very successful one." Autumn shrugged. "I mean she's still proud of me for being successful, even if it's a successful bad guy."

"Your family sounds fun."

Autumn studied him. "I'm guessing yours isn't?"

He opened his mouth, then shook his head. He wasn't quite ready. "I had an idea, for how we get around your issue of not wanting to tell men you date that you're a sub."

"Is it date a Dom?" she asked dryly.

"That would work, but I had another idea."

"This conversation has gone so far off the rails." She took a sip…no, that was a gulp…of wine.

"It's because I'm stalling," he acknowledged.

"Daniel, we only met yesterday. It's okay if you want to wait to tell me whatever it is."

"No. Waiting won't make it any easier."

"All right, then." She settled back in the chaise. "I'll just sit here and drink wine. Take your time."

That made him smile. It was so damn easy to talk to her.

And suddenly the words were there.

"BDSM is how, and where, I channel my need for control," he said. "Before I found BDSM, well, and to be fair before my years of therapy, I had to be in control. I *had* to. I grew up with… with no control, so as an adult I swung the other way."

She watched him with compassion, but no pity. "I'm sorry, that must have been hard."

"I don't mean that I just had a chaotic childhood." Time to take the plunge. "I actually grew up in a cult, living in an isolated compound."

"Holy shit. Daniel, are you serious?"

"Yep. My mom joined the cult when she was nineteen. I was born there. My father was probably the cult leader—he called himself 'the apostle.' His thing was that the cult was a church. His church. And they were the only true christians."

"How original."

"It gets better. He 'married' most of the women, and girls, at one point or another. Marriages that lasted only for as long as he wanted to fuck them. There were other men, all older, living there, but I'm pretty sure he was my father, and the father of most of the other kids born into the cult."

"Daniel…" Autumn scooted forward, so she was sitting on the end of her chaise, close enough to reach him.

"He used them, the kids, to manipulate and control the women. Some weeks children were pampered and loved, the next used as literal whipping boys to keep the adults in line. Some weeks they had school every day, the next there was no school at all, and the week after that they were forced to study twenty hours a day.

"The children slept in different places each night, depending on his whims. Sometimes inside, but on the floor with no blankets, sometimes in lovely soft beds. On bad nights, the kids were locked out of all the homes. Mothers would look out the windows at their children, but they never opened the doors. Not if he said they couldn't."

Autumn grabbed his hands, squeezing them fiercely. "I'm so sorry."

"It's okay, because it was a long time ago. I separated that kid from who I am now."

"I noticed you said 'the children' and 'they.' Not 'me' or 'us.'"

"I've learned to do that." He raised a brow. "It made my congressional testimony easier."

CHAPTER 17

She blinked. "Your…what?"

He laughed, needing the moment of levity.

"Next is the part where I tell my story." He laced his fingers together, looked at his thumbs. "I was kicked out of the cult when I was thirteen. I was 'impure in the faith', meaning I started to fight back and question his bullshit. I'd gotten a hold of some fiction books that were tucked in the very bottom of a donated box of school supplies. Finding out that the world outside wasn't the hellscape the apostle described, reading stories where the man I was expected to revere had more in common with the villains than the heroes…that changed things for me."

Usually he sped through this part, but he found himself telling her things that he normally didn't talk about.

"I barely remember my childhood. Only a few memories are vivid." He swallowed then shook his head, to push those few vivid memories, all of which were horrific, to the back of his mind.

"It's common with children who experience early trauma to have fuzzy memories," he said. "But I do remember how it felt when I finally realized that the world was so much bigger than I thought. I felt hopeful, for the first time in my life."

Autumn was biting the inside of her cheek, he could tell from the set of her jaw. He had a feeling she was fighting not to cry, and damn it he loved her for that, for not turning this into a situation where he had to comfort her, which had happened in the past.

He cleared his throat, and decided to power through the rest. "The compound was in the Arizona desert. When they kicked me out I had to walk. It was sheer fucking luck the direction I picked was towards a town and not deeper into the desert.

"I walked for days. Didn't die of dehydration, exposure...I should have. But I didn't. And when I reached the closest town, it was like arriving in Oz. A world full of color. Of people who rushed to help me. A stranger who saw me stumbling along and got me in his car, brought me to the little hospital. The nurses and doctors who called in social workers, and then the authorities.

"These people listened to me. Every one of them asked if I was okay, what I needed. They wanted to hear my story, and once I started talking, I wouldn't shut up. Wouldn't stop demanding that the apostle be stopped. That these strangers who had helped me help the other children too."

"You were just a child. It shouldn't have been up to you to prod authorities to do what was right."

"I was a child who figured out, real fucking fast, that my words had power. That I had power."

"It takes some of us a long time to realize that. Or to accept it once we realize it." She raised their linked hands, kissed his knuckles.

"It, of course, wasn't that easy. The sheriff went out there to talk to them, but they claimed I'd run away. That I was a bad seed. I refused to follow their rules, and therefore wasn't welcome in their community—all of which was true. They said they would happily sign the paperwork making me an emancipated minor."

"Your...your mother said that?"

"Yes."

"I'm so sorry."

"I accepted a long time ago that her need for validation was far more important to her than caring for a child."

"The sheriff had to know they were lying."

"The best they could do was to charge my mother with child abandonment for kicking me out. They tried a sex crimes case, to get him for statutory rape, based on my statements."

"Were you... I'm sorry, I shouldn't have asked that."

"No, it's okay. I wasn't raped, wasn't abused in that way."

Daniel took a moment to gather his thoughts.

"The apostle had sex with all the women and girls. The girls, children," he stressed the word, "he raped...many were his own daughters. Some of them were also 'married' off to the 'elders' and 'counselors' who were the few other men he allowed to stay. Meaning they were raped by them too. My statements were enough for them to go out and question the girls, do welfare checks."

"Let me guess, the girls said nothing was wrong."

"Yes."

"The sheriff would have dropped it, just because of lack of resources and time, but like I said, I wouldn't shut up. And I had backup. The god-damn saint of a social worker who got my case. She was handed this insane, feral teenage boy, and she had my back every step of the way. Eventually we made enough noise that the local FBI office stepped in."

"Ha, so there are feds in this story."

"Yes, but none of them are undercover at a BDSM club." He quirked a brow.

That made her smile, just as he'd hoped.

"There wasn't much the feds could do, either," he went on.

"My word wasn't enough. It was me against a whole group of adults. Which story is more reasonable—a pissed off teenager who didn't like his strict upbringing was making shit up, or a small, almost Orthodox Church with a pure, humble image was actually a cult?"

"Honestly, it's easier to believe they were a cult."

"I agree, but in court, their story was more reasonable."

This part of the story was oft repeated, the words flowing easily.

"Still, the local agents knew, and believed, something was wrong. The problem was they couldn't prove it, and had nothing actionable but my testimony. That's when they asked Agent Rand Salford to look at the case. He spent two days just listening as I ranted and raved. Then, he made it his mission to take them down. He started with the IRS."

"Ah, the IRS. I get audited every year."

"You do?" Daniel raised an eyebrow, then glanced around. "Uh, what do you do?"

"I play a game. It's a high stakes game, that I'm very good at." She had a sly little smile on that made him want to kiss her.

Everything made him want to kiss her.

"You're a professional poker player," he guessed.

"Hedge fund manager."

"Damn. Well, that explains the view."

"Enough about my morally gray career. The IRS got them? The cult?"

"No. What they did was open a case, which allowed them to audit the paperwork the apostle had turned in to have the cult recognized as a church."

"And therefore tax exempt?"

"Exactly."

"Like how they got Al Capone for tax evasion."

He liked that she wasn't focused on the shitty personal parts of the story. Later—months, years later, he might let that little boy out of the box at the back of his mind and tell her about some of the pain he still carried. She could be trusted with that. He knew it the way he knew that the sun would rise again tomorrow.

"Not quite," he said, bringing his mind back to the story. "You see the IRS is really cautious about denying church status to organizations. They have to err on the side of caution."

"But if it was a cult, couldn't they do something?"

"What's the difference between a church and a cult?"

Autumn opened her mouth, frowned, then made a frustrated noise.

"Exactly. It's easy when you've got people promising the space ships are on their way. But one of the technical definitions of a cult is a group whose beliefs and practices are regarded by others as strange."

"Oh...That's a problem, because how do you define 'strange'?"

"You see the issue."

Autumn squeezed his hands, then stood. He watched her as she walked to the kitchen, grabbed another wine stem, poured him a very full glass, and brought it over.

"If we're discussing the technical definition of cults, we should be drinking," she declared.

"Fair enough." He waited for her to raise her glass, tapped it with his own, then took a sip. "I'll cut to the chase. Usually when I give these talks, it's to law enforcement seminars."

"Wait, so you *are* a fed. Just not undercover."

"No, not a fed. Wait until the end of the story."

"Fine." Autumn laced her fingers through his, using her other hand to raise her wine glass to her lips.

"The IRS investigation gave Agent Salford access to current financial records. And this is where that man's genius really shows. You see, the church had a business selling ceramics. Handmade stuff that they sold online. The website had a whole section about how each piece was special, hand made by someone who'd devoted their life to god. There was a gimmick about how the members would go out and pray in the desert at dawn, then bring back handfuls of sand that were full of the 'Holy Spirit' and mix them into the clay."

Autumn's lip curled. "Ugh."

"People ate that bullshit up. Well, Agent Salford used the pictures on that site, along with the information I was able to give him, to definitively identify three women in particular who were featured in photos and listed as the artists on the church business site."

"And who were they?"

Even now, the next part of the story made him smile.

"What they weren't, was adults. They were all minors."

Autumn raised a brow. "Wait, did he get them for violating child labor laws?"

"Yep, and then, he took it one step further. He got them for human trafficking."

Autumn sucked in air. "The cult leader was forcing the kids into prostitution?"

Daniel shook his head. "When people say human trafficking, they think of sex workers, sex trafficking, but it's defined as using force, fraud, or coercion to exploit people for sex acts, or labor. He got them on labor trafficking."

"So the girls wouldn't, couldn't, admit to the physical and sexual abuse, but Agent Salford got them to talk about being forced to make ceramic mugs."

"He didn't have to. It was all right there in the financial records. The accounting was set up to say the artists were all full-time volunteers, who were given food and lodging in exchange for their documented full-time volunteer efforts.

"But they were children. Children have limits as to how much they can work, even if it's as a volunteer. It is severe psychological manipulation to make provision of shelter and food, both of which children have a right to, dependent on a child's labor output. Therefore, the church was guilty of violating child labor laws, human trafficking, and child neglect. The charges stuck, and most of the adults were convicted."

"He managed to turn their cutesy bullshit store into evidence against them. Damn. That's good."

"And he did it all using their own financial records. Because you see, Rand Salford wasn't with the FBI human trafficking division. He was with white collar financial crimes. He was a forensic accountant."

He knew he was smiling, and she answered his smile with one of her own.

"The apostle—and by the way, I call him that because I refuse to say his name—was eventually prosecuted for pedophilia and rape, when some of the girls came forward, after they'd been out of the cult for a while, and learned what was normal."

"Good. I'm glad he had to pay for those crimes."

"And the day I turned 18 I changed my name. Daniel after the main character in *The Shadow of the Wind*. The first book I found in that box and read. And Randall after Agent Randall 'Rand' Salford."

She squeezed his hand. "You're a forensic accountant, aren't you?"

"Yes."

"Can I tell you something?" she asked.

"Of course."

"And I want you to really listen."

"I'm listening," he assured her.

"You're amazing. You're kind and sexy and smart." She set her glass aside and then slid off the chaise, onto her knees in front of him. She kissed their linked fingers, then raised their hands to her face, rubbing her cheek against his knuckles. "You had every right to tell me to stop being such a headache when I walked off. You didn't. You helped me deal with my own shit. Made me feel safe. You are, quite simply, amazing."

Daniel looked down at Autumn. The deep V of her shirt gave him an almost perfect view of her breasts. He wanted to reach down and grasp her gently by the throat. Order her to open her mouth, just so he could imagine what it would look like when his cock slid between her lips.

Wanted to slide his hand into her shirt, tug her breast out so it was exposed, so he could play with her nipple.

He wouldn't, couldn't, because now she knew about his past…but she didn't know his secret.

"Autumn…don't. I can't touch you. Not until you know…"

"Know what?"

"That I'm a monster."

CHAPTER 18

It took everything she had not to burst into tears. To sob for the little boy he'd been. A child who never had a chance to be a child, who had reinvented himself. Taken a new name and followed in the footsteps of a man who he'd seen as a hero.

Everything about him, from his easy self-confidence to the calm way he'd handled her emotional responses, spoke of a man who was sure of himself and his place in the world. It must have taken a lot of work for him to get there, and she wanted to stand up and start clapping. Shout "Bravo" because, damn it, he needed to be celebrated for what he'd overcome.

The smile was gone from his face. His expression had become unreadable. "I can't touch you. Not until you know..."

Her stomach clenched. "Know what?"

"That I'm a monster."

"No." Her denial was vehement. He wouldn't let her think badly about herself, and she was going to do the same for him.

But when he shook his head she stopped, her next protest dying on her tongue.

"This is the part where you find out I'm a liar." He tugged

his hand free of hers and stood, leaving her kneeling, facing an empty chair.

"My secret isn't what happened to me as a child. That's public record. I testified at the trials—which took years to make it to court—when I was adult, so my name, my new name is listed. You could google me and find it."

"You said before that how you appear is a lie. Daniel, it's not. I get it, you modeled yourself on the FBI agent who you saw slay a monster. That's not all that different from what the rest of us do. No one tells you that fake it until you make it doesn't mean that you'll stop feeling like a fake once you actually do make it."

He stood at the window, hands in his pockets. His waistcoat hugged his trim waist, emphasized the breath of his shoulders. He looked like a CEO, a titan of industry taking a moment at the end of a long day.

"You aren't defined by who you were as a child, or what happened to you," she said softly.

He was out there somewhere, in the shadows, a child who had never made it to adulthood, his identity erased at 18 when the boy he'd been shed that ragged, battered identity to become the first iteration of the man he now was.

"I'm a Dom because I need control. I don't just like it. I *need* it. I've learned to accept that there are situations and people I cannot control. It took a long time, but I accepted it."

Autumn got off her knees and perched on the end of the chaise. "Well, you did a good job compartmentalizing, because on first impressions you're an easy-going, insightful, and compassionate man."

"Thanks to literal years of therapy."

She waited for him to continue, but he just stood there, looking out at the night.

"Daniel." Autumn rose, crossing her arms. "Enough with the dramatic staring into the darkness. What am I missing?" A thought occurred to her. "Did your therapist tell you that being a Dom was a bad idea? Because of your issues with control?"

"I told him I liked to be in control in the bedroom, but didn't open it up for a full discussion. Never mentioned D/s, or joining Las Palmas."

"Why not?"

"Because I convinced myself that I didn't need to. That bottling up this need, letting it out only when I'm doing D/s, was okay. That the rules of BDSM, being in the club…that was enough structure to contain my need."

She sorted through what he was saying, both actual words and the unsaid, the subtext that was written in the tense lines of his body. "So each of us is using BDSM, and Las Palmas, as a lockbox. A place where we keep a part of ourselves we don't want anyone else to see, or know about."

Finally, he turned away from the window. "I knew exactly what you were talking about last night, when we were sitting in the grass, and you said that you didn't want to mix romance with D/s."

"And for you…" The analytical part of her brain made a connection she hadn't seen before, and the realization caused a soft, heavy feeling to pool in her gut. "Oh. You don't want anyone outside of the club to know you like BDSM, because you're worried that they'll wonder why you like it, given your past."

His shoulders dropped, and he stared at the floor for a long moment. When he looked up, he was smiling, but it wasn't his normal smile. The smile that she found so damn attractive. It was a cruel twist of his lips.

"Knowing now that I'm the son of a cult leader pedophile abuser, aren't you at least a little alarmed that I'm a sexual sadist?"

He was ready for her to deny it. She could see it in the way he was standing. If she'd say 'no', that she trusted him, he'd point out that she just met him.

Time to flip the script.

"Of course I'm worried about it. I'm not an idiot."

Daniel blinked.

"Why do I like having men hit me? I got enough love as a child. But clearly something in me is broken, and it was before my exes fucked me up."

"Autumn…"

"So fine, we're clichés. I'm a successful woman in a predominately male setting. I'm perfectly in control and even aggressive in my day-to-day life, but I need to be topped in the bedroom. This is hardly an earth-shatteringly unique profile. It's why I'm pretty sure half the other managers at my firm see Dommes on the weekends. They need the same release I do.

"And you had a legitimately terrible childhood and overcompensated as an adult by trying to control everything. Therapy helped you deal with most of it, but you still like dominating women in the bedroom."

"You're oversimplifying it," he warned.

"Am I? Or is it my turn to help you see what's really going on in your head?"

"I shouldn't have…I don't talk about this with my subs."

"Your sub? Back it up, blue eyes." She rose, stalking towards him, putting herself within arm's reach. "I'm not yours."

He inhaled, eyes wide, nostrils flaring.

"Ohhh, don't like that, do you?" She smirked at him.

"Watch it, lover."

"Listen to me, *Sir*." She used the term to get his attention. "You're not a Dom because of some genetic predisposition to use and hurt people. You're a Dom because being in control is the only way you can be sure you'll be able to protect me."

She'd meant to say "protect *them*." Protect subs in general. She swallowed hard and brazened through it.

"If all you'd wanted was a willing body, you wouldn't have come after me. Wouldn't have sat with me outside, and talked to me. Helped me see that it was fear not hypocrisy at the root of my issue."

For the first time he looked uncomfortable, turning his head away. Autumn reached up and cupped his cheek, forcing him to face her.

"You, Daniel Randall, are a protector. You're a good man."

"If I was—"

"Don't finish that sentence, because if you say something stupid like 'if I were good I wouldn't enjoy giving boob hickies' I'm going to toss my wine in your face."

He snorted in startled amusement.

"And if you're broken for being a sadist, then the other side of that coin is that I must be just as broken to be a masochist. But you already told me that I'm not broken. Are you going to contradict yourself?"

"I think that's a logical fallacy."

Autumn dropped her hands from his face, wrapping them around his waist and laying her head on his shoulder. "You've always been a protector. And if that need to protect means you're controlling in the bedroom, well then I guess the ways we're fucked up, the ways we're wounded, somehow match."

His arms came around her, his cheek resting on her hair.

They stayed that way, just holding one another, for a long time.

"You need a rug. The floor is hard." Daniel tipped his head back against the seat of the sofa so he was looking at her.

"Normally people don't sit on the floor." Autumn held up a piece of melon. He opened his mouth and she popped it in.

It was nearly 3a.m. but she wasn't tired. Neither, apparently, was Daniel. About an hour ago they'd both gotten hungry, so she'd made a quick tray of fruit, crackers, and cheese. When they brought it to the couch, rather than sitting beside her, he'd opted for the floor.

His waistcoat was with his jacket, draped over one of the counter chairs. His tie hung loose around his neck.

For the past few hours they'd talked. About their jobs—hers in the world of finance, his as a forensic accountant, and one of the go-to expert witnesses for the Justice Department. He couldn't talk about many of his cases, since there were gag orders in place, but he told her what he could.

They had a funny moment when they realized that if Autumn did ever decide to turn to a life of crime, it would probably be someone like Daniel the Feds brought in to look at her financial records.

She'd had a brief interrogation/prison role play fantasy, but was keeping that to herself for now.

They'd talked about college and their best friends, which had led to her remembering to text Summer that she was still alive and that she had in fact brought Daniel home with her.

They talked about their favorite restaurants and movies. Their hobbies—she crocheted, which had made him laugh, but she knew it wasn't at her, rather because it was so unexpected.

He surfed and was teaching himself guitar. She'd launched into a long diatribe on how he was basically a walking young adult novel hero. Handsome, protective, wealthy, with two sexy hobbies and a tragic past.

He'd laughed so hard he inhaled wine and she had to pound on his back.

Now the conversation had died down, settling into a companionable silence.

"What are you thinking about?" She slid her hand through his hair, lightly scratching his scalp, which he seemed to like.

"You."

"Aww, that's cute, but we're pretty well past the point where we need cute pickup lines."

Daniel rolled onto his knees, turning to face her. "It wasn't a line."

"All right…what about me?"

"I was thinking that you're probably going to panic a little when our first official date turns in to me topping you in the bedroom."

She froze, every muscle in her body tensing. The languid warmth of their companionship turned into something else. Raw, hot need. It terrified her.

"Probably," she agreed, sounding a little breathless.

Daniel scooted closer, his hips against the front of the couch. He reached out, planting his hands on either side of her shoulders. She had her legs curled up to the side, mermaid style, so she was now trapped. "Your trauma is more recent than mine."

"Having two boyfriends react shittily to my kink isn't even in the same league as what you—"

He shook his head, cutting her off with a decisive, "No. We don't qualify or compare trauma."

"You're right." She shook her hair back. "So if you're going to top me after our date, are you going to wind up in a guilt/shame spiral when you leave marks on my ass?"

"You do remember that I have no problem marking you…or punishing you."

She hummed in acknowledgment.

"Imagining your ass with a handprint mark on it isn't making me feel bad, or guilty."

"What is it making you feel?" she murmured.

He leaned in, gaze traveling down her face to her cleavage. "It's making me feel like turning you over my knee right here. Right now."

Yes. Oh yes, touch me. Spank me.

"Nope," she gasped, surprising herself. But as hot as this conversation was, this felt like a date, and her instincts were screaming at her not to let it veer into BDSM territory.

"We're...we're in the living room and we were just having a nice night and, and..."

"Calm down, lover." He dropped his hands. "We'll set limits. You only want to play when we're physically in the bedroom? We can do that. We can have rules. A signal."

"Wait, wait, are we doing this?" She gestured between them. "Are we...dating? Are we going to apply to be a bonded pair at the club?" It was the term Las Palmas used to cover partners who had a formal relationship. It was an umbrella term that included collaring and a few other things.

"I could say something like, 'Do you believe in soul mates?' Or 'Do you think it's possible to fall in love with someone after only a day?' But you said no cheesy pickup lines, so I won't say either of those things."

"This might end badly," she warned.

"It might. Or maybe we'll die together side by side when we're ninety."

Autumn threw her arms around his neck, hugging him tight. It was an awkward embrace, with him bent over while he was still kneeling on the floor. It didn't matter. She just needed to hold him.

"This is terrifying," she murmured, "because if it doesn't work..."

"We'll break each other's hearts." Daniel slid his hands under her ass, and hauled her off the couch so she was sitting astride his legs. "If it happens, it happens. But neither of us is afraid of a little pain."

She looked into his eyes, and realized she would rather risk her heart for the chance to love, and be loved by, this man. Maybe he'd turn out to be like Mike, and start expecting her to be submissive in all aspects of life. Or find her needs boring after a while. From him, those attitudes would hurt far worse than it had with her other exes.

She would take that risk, for him.

With him.

Autumn shook her hair off her shoulders.

"Well, I'm not afraid. But I'm a masochist." She raised her brows and gave him a once over—not that she could see much of him, seated on his lap. "Maybe you dish it out, but can't take it."

"Ohh, are you calling me a pussy?"

"No, because pussies are tough. I'm calling you a…a scrotum maybe?"

Daniel threw back his head and laughed. The sound vibrated her whole body. When he stopped laughing and looked at her with that amazing smile, she tumbled that last little bit. Falling wholly and fearlessly in love.

"I almost forgot to tell you my idea. How we get around you're not wanting to tell men you date you're submissive," he said.

"Pretty sure that ship sailed."

"Play along." With an impressive show of strength he grabbed her waist and lifted her back onto the couch. Then he rose to his feet. As she watched, he rebuttoned his collar, while walking to the big glass wall, which he then used as a mirror to retie his tie.

When he turned back, he was no longer just Daniel, the man who'd sat on her floor and talked to her for hours. Or Daniel the man who'd sat on wet grass to listen to her shameful feelings.

This was the Daniel who'd mercilessly worked her body. Who'd demanded her submission, and rewarded her with pleasure and pain.

He stopped in front of her and cleared his throat. "Autumn,

as you know we've been dating for several months now, but haven't slept together."

She smirked. "A bit of an info dump, but okay, I'll play along." She cleared her throat. "Yes, and you're a wonderful boyfriend, Daniel."

"And we're definitely attracted to one another."

"Oh yes, and we've had some good heavy petting make-out sessions."

He mock-glared at her, which made her lips twitch.

"The reason," he went on, "that we haven't slept together, is that there's something I need to tell you."

Autumn studied his face, trying to figure out where he was going with this.

"I enjoy…no, need…to engage in a type of sex that you might find alarming."

She raised her brows as she realized what he was doing. He was flipping the script, as she had.

"Is it butt stuff?" she asked with mock concern.

"Actually, it is. But I'm not just talking about anal sex." He stalked closer, reached up, and started to undo the tie he'd just knotted. "I'm a sexual dominant. That means I like to be in charge in the bedroom. It means I'd like to tie you up so you're helpless, and then touch you. Touch every inch of you, however I want."

He jerked the tie free of his shirt collar. She licked her upper lip.

"And it's a little more than that. I like all the letters in BDSM, not just the D/s. That means I want to do kinky, taboo things to you."

"Things like what?" Her nipples were hard inside her bra and her pussy was wet.

Daniel smirked, clearly having noticed her sudden fidgets.

"Like spanking you."

"Because I was bad?"

"Maybe. Sometimes I'll spank you just because I want to. I'll use more than my hand. Maybe I'll paddle your ass, or use a flogger."

Autumn clenched her teeth, but that didn't silence her moan of mingled arousal and need.

"And I'll spank more than just your very nice ass." He grabbed one end of the tie in each fist, snapping it taut.

She watched his hands, as if hypnotized, as he began to wind the tie around his palm.

"I'm telling you this, because I'm hoping you'd be interested in trying this with me. If you don't want to, that's fine. If you're not sure what I'm talking about, I can send you links, articles you can read about BDSM, and all its various iterations."

The length of the tie was wrapped around his left fist. He used his right hand to roll up his left shirt cuff. Damn he had sexy forearms.

"If you don't want—"

Autumn jumped to her feet, standing on the couch. "Yes."

"Yes?" he asked.

"Yes, I want to try." She shook her head. "No more role play, you know I want this."

"I know, but I wanted to give you a chance to be the one who was asked, rather than having to do the asking."

"Bring that sexy forearm over here and kiss me."

Daniel took two big steps, and wrapped his arms around her ass. She hooked her legs around his waist, cupped his face in her hands, and kissed him.

Their first kiss. A kiss between two people who knew each other. Who in less than forty-eight hours had shared more than some couples ever managed.

She kissed him like she trusted him, and she did with both her body and soul.

Kissed him with everything she had. With all the passion and desire and hope she had to offer.

Kissed him as a promise, a pledge, to give him everything. To be his partner, his lover, his submissive.

Kissed him like she loved him, because she did.

EPILOGUE

"What about O?" Mikel asked.

Leo glanced at the blank checklist on the table considering the items on the list that began with that letter. O included orgasm denial. He looked at Gabriela.

The four of them had created Las Palmas together, and while technically himself, Mikel, and Faith were the overseers, Gabriela, his wife, lover, and bonded submissive, was an equal partner in the ownership of Las Palmas.

Leo looked up. "Mikel, can you look in that drawer and see if there's a spare butterfly vibrator?"

Leo felt it when Gabriela glanced at him. Mikel's lips twitched, and he reached back to open one of the many cabinet drawers.

This office was the least elegant room in the club. It was where they kept all the paperwork, sorted mail, and also where they kept overflow stock of the sex toys they bought by the case.

Mikel pulled out a flat package with the picture of a purple butterfly and an artistic silhouette of a woman's hips.

Leo accepted it, and without looking at Gabriela said, "Strip."

Without protest, she stood and stripped off the leggings and t-shirt she wore, with nothing on underneath. He'd spanked her several times already, just because he could, because she liked it, and because though they rarely played out in public on weekends when the club was full, she did enjoy being put on display.

"Mikel, will you work her nipples for me?" Leo asked casually.

Gabriela barely managed to hold back a moan. She couldn't stop her nipples from hardening in response to his order.

Mikel scooted back and tugged her down onto his lap. Gabriela obediently spread her legs. Mikel brought her arms together behind her, then made her lie back against him, her arms between their bodies arching her back up, her breasts lifted.

Mikel cruelly flicked her nipples, eliciting little hisses of pain.

Leo watched attentively even as he accepted the package of baby wipes Faith handed him and started to clean the new toy.

"O," Faith said. "Anyone have any strong opinions?"

"Outdoor, Orgasm, Oral." Mikel punctuated each word with a pinch or twist to Gabby's tits.

Leo rose from his chair only to kneel and slide the two loops of elastic over Gabby's feet. When he had them to her knees he nodded to Mikel, who pushed her up.

He slid the bands up to her hips. The small, curved purple vibrator rested on her vulva. He spread her pussy lips, and nestled the vibrator in place over her clit.

With a casual pat to her pussy, he resumed his seat. "Clothes on," he ordered.

He waited until she had her leggings halfway up her legs before he flicked the control, turning the vibrator on. She nearly stumbled, and shot him a dirty look.

He raised one brow, that small gesture promising punishment.

"The question is, who do we think will put on a good show?" Faith asked.

"Who will craft an outdoor orgasm denial scene so depraved and torturous that every sub in the club will be terrified they're next?" Mikel added.

"Edge," Gabriela gasped.

Leo turned the vibrator off.

"Damn it," she moaned.

Leo looked at the membership files spread out on the table. He considered what his friends had said, then picked one up, holding it aloft.

"What do you think?"

Faith nodded. Mikel grinned.

Leo turned the vibrator back on, and looked at his wife. "You don't have permission to come."

He knew she hated orgasm denial, but hated it in the way of a submissive. Where she hated it, but responded beautifully to it.

He selected a second file. This one belonged to a submissive who most likely would not respond as obediently to the frustration of denial.

Faith nodded in approval, stacked the files together, and went to write the names under the letter O.

Beside him, Gabriela hissed. "Edge."

Leo turned the vibrator off, and smiled.

Love sexy stories set in BDSM clubs?
Check out the *Orchid Club* series, starting with
San Francisco Longing

Oh wait! How about a free ebook?

Sign up for Lila's Newsletter to get San Francisco Longing, as well as three other great stories, totally free.

Get four FREE ebooks when you join Lila's newsletter!
Go to
www.liladubois.net
and click on the "Free Books" link at the top of the page.

A NOTE FROM LILA...

I never intended this series to be romance. My original plan was for all the checklist books to be straight erotica. Each story would take place over the course of a weekend and focus on the items and toys related to that letter.

Some (possibly many) of the books ended up being far more erotic romance than erotica. Those pesky characters kept developing feelings for one another. This book is both a romance and a story about learning to accept yourself.

Whether you prefer spicy romance, or straight erotica, I hope you enjoyed Daniel and Autumn's story. If you'd like to discuss with like-minded readers, you can join the Checklist Club Facebook group.

AND IF YOU'RE LOOKING FOR SOME RECOMMENDATIONS FOR WHAT TO READ NEXT, CHECK OUT THESE SERIES.

- For BDSM club-based books that are definitely romance: Orchid Club trilogies.

A NOTE FROM LILA...

- For BDSM with a rockabilly vibe: Undone Lovers.
- For secret club romantic suspense, try the Trinity Masters and Masters's Admiralty series I co-write with Mari Carr.

I hope you and your loved ones are safe and healthy.
~Lila

ABOUT THE AUTHOR

Lila Dubois is an award winning, multi-published, bestselling author of erotic, paranormal and fantasy romance. Her book *J is for...*, the tenth book in the bestselling checklist series, won the 2019 National Readers' Choice Award. Additionally, she's been nominated for the RT Book Reviews Erotic Novella of the Year for *Undone Rebel* and the Golden Flogger.

Having spent extensive time in France, Egypt, Turkey, Ireland and England Lila speaks five languages, none of them (including English) fluently. Lila lives in California with her own Irish Farm Boy and loves receiving email from readers.

Visit Lila online:
www.liladubois.net
author@liladubois.net

Printed in Great Britain
by Amazon